The Far
Distant
Mountains

Malania E. Reynolds

THREE SKILLET

The Far Distant Mountains

Copyright © 2016 by Malania E. Reynolds

Edited by Farley Dunn
Cover art by Farley Dunn

 THREE SKILLET

www.ThreeSkilletPublishing.com

ISBN: 978-1-943189-23-6

One

$\sim\!\!\!\!\diamond\!\!\!\!\sim$

"All aboard!" shouted the burly train conductor, as he walked slowly toward the crowd of people waiting to board the train. His flat-topped blue cap and stiffly-cuffed jacket gave him a pompous air, but it also pulled the crowd's attention his way. Up and down the platform, formally-dressed men stepped sprightly toward Fuller Hadley's car, more than one with a leather case in one hand. The women at their sides wore wide-brimmed hats decorated with feathers and unusual artificial flowers. More than one carried a parasol in a gloved hand. A few children tugged at their parents' coats as they made their way to the First Class coach, but more were further down the train, with whole families entering the Second Class cars that would soon be blasted with the engine smoke and coal ash from the train's massive steam boilers.

Fuller Hadley nodded and dropped the cigar he had in his hand; he stamped on it with his foot, putting out the flame, and followed an especially harried-looking couple up the stairs. The husband dropped a patterned hatbox. It fell open to reveal wrapped items of food, and his wife scolded him as he retrieved them from the steps. Fuller stood patiently as they sorted out their belongings. The man motioned Fuller to go around, and as he moved to do so, he was jostled from behind by a heavyset, blustery man, knocking his hat from his head.

"Look where you're going," the man muttered, as if it was Fuller's fault. Fuller stooped to pick up his hat, and the man shoved his way past him without further words.

"Hmmmph." Fuller was hard-pressed to let the rude passenger go without retaliation, but he'd seen men like him before. And the ride on the train was to be a long one. It wouldn't do to make an enemy of a man he might be forced to sit with for a hundred miles. He found his seat, laid his medical bag, coat, newspapers and valise beside him and positioned himself next to the window. A wagon traveling at a great speed barreled up to the station wall, a last-minute arrival, and a young woman and man cast themselves to the ground. The man reached in the wagon for a couple of large cases and a colorful carpetbag, all the while calling something to the woman. She held her hat firmly on her head, pressed some cash into the wagon driver's hand and hurried to the conductor standing near the door. Through the mud-splattered window Fuller could see their lips move but couldn't hear what they said. The conductor in his blue cap motioned for the man to hurry, and he took the carpet bag in hand to aid the couple in their ascent up the steps. The driver of the wagon turned the vehicle and headed back in the direction of town with an unconcerned air.

Fuller smiled and looked away. A whistle blew, and he felt

the tug of the wheels as the engine began to pull the train from the station. He settled more comfortably in his seat and saw a small crowd of twenty or so people waving from the front of the building. He heard the sound of a woman's laughter and looked up to see the couple from the wagon coming down the aisle toward him.

"I told you, Sweet, that you should hurry, but no, you had to dawdle like always. We almost missed the train." The man struggled to keep upright with the rocking movement of the coach. He dropped one case and struggled to regain a hold on it. After a moment, he sighed and left it for the time being, moving on after his wife.

"I know, Sam, I'm sorry, but I had to make sure I had my ticket, didn't I?" The woman laughed again, and they passed on down the aisle. Fuller smiled, certain he'd never be so foolish as to misplace his own train ticket. After two minutes or so, the man returned. He retrieved his bag, and catching Fuller's eye, he chuckled and shook his head, remarking as he passed by, "At least she's a good cook."

The train began to pick up speed, and Fuller felt the movement of the car and saw the buildings slowly disappear from sight as they left the town behind. He fleetingly thought of his own luggage and hoped he'd packed everything. He saw a flock of sheep standing in a corral and wondered if they were being sold. A loud voice came from the back of the car, and he turned his head. It was the heavyset, blustery man arguing with the conductor. He couldn't help overhearing them as their voices increased in volume. The man objected to the seat he'd been given. The door opened, and he pushed angrily through to the next car. Quiet was once more restored, and the only sound was the occasional burst of steam or the screech of the horn.

Fuller gazed with wistful eyes at the passing scenery as the shadow of the train crawled along beside him. The long prairie journey seemed endless, and he was tired. His time in New York had been filled planning his itinerary west with the assistance of a helpful clerk at the railroad terminal and shopping for small gifts for his relatives. He closed his eyes, but the memories kept repeating themselves in his mind. He'd left New York on a rainy, cold day in late February and arrived a few days later in Indianapolis for a visit with his relatives. His Great-Uncle Claude Edison proved to be a shrunken, shell of a man, with a bald head and rheumy eyes. With Fuller's medical expertise, he evaluated him as he'd been taught to do, recognizing the man's serious heart condition. Claude, however, lived with his oldest daughter, Claudette, and her husband, and when Fuller had suggested a more thorough examination by the man's personal physician, Claudette had demurred, and her husband had backed her. There was nothing Fuller could do about it, for he was just a visitor, and he let the matter go.

For the rest of the visit, Fuller had enjoyed a drink and a smoke with Percy Seldon, Claudette's husband, a large-boned, affable sort, well-versed in the literary works of America and Great Britain.

Following his father's request, he'd changed trains and traveled on to Topeka, Kansas, to visit with his father's old employer, Ned Baldwin. He looked again at the fast-moving shadows on the fields of grass and sighed as he remembered the sweet face of Sally Baldwin, Ned's granddaughter, introduced to Fuller as the eldest child of Baldwin's second son, Tom. She was a lovely girl, and he could grow to love her if he were to remain in Kansas, but the staid existence of the eastern states wasn't for him.

Perched high above the river, the white multi-storied house had rung with laughter, music and barking dogs that first night of his visit. Baldwin stood on his porch and extoled the virtues of a fine life in a prosperous city, exclaiming that it was something every man could long for, but few could achieve. Then he told Fuller that building his new home the previous year on an untamed tract of land had been exhausting, and he only undertook the family's move at his wife's pleading request. His wife and granddaughter, dressed in their elegant finery, laughed at Ned's remarks, but Fuller saw the seriousness in the man's eyes. It was only after the meal that he'd a chance for a serious talk with his host.

"Sit down, Fuller. Please. Would you like a snort?" Ned Baldwin poured a small amount of port in a glass and turned to Fuller, holding the bottle aloft.

"Yes, Mr. Baldwin, I'd like a drink. Thank you." Fuller looked around at the shelves filled with books of all sizes and shapes. The heavy drapes on the window kept out the dying rays of the sun, and the room was dim except for a glowing lamp on the desk and a lighted pole lamp standing in the corner. He took the glass held out to him and sighed.

He watched as Baldwin sat in his heavy leather chair behind his massive wooden desk. Fuller observed that in spite of his parchment-gray skin and the crinkles around his eyes, the man must have carried himself well and been filled with vigor in his youth.

"The doctor says I'm too old and frail to drink, so I hide in here at night and hope the wife or one of the grandchildren doesn't come in." Baldwin laughed, finished his drink and brought his attention to Fuller. "You're a doctor yourself, so's you understand how a man needs some stimulation." He coughed and squinted at Fuller. "Your pa was about your age the first time I saw him. He was strong of character and courageous. I was drawn to him immediately. The years have gone so swiftly, and the days of cross-country stage travel long passed, but I still remember how he took to the new challenge with the boldness of a man twice his age."

He paused a moment, and Fuller finished his drink and set the glass on the small table beside his chair. As though his movement awakened Baldwin from a trance, the man blinked and sat up straighter.

"Well, you don't want to hear about the days of long ago. I have enough sons and sons-in-law and grandsons to appreciate the modern man. Tell me, Fuller, what're your plans for the future? Are you going to settle in Colorado and start a medical practice of your own?"

"I've thought about it, sir. But, somehow the idea of working in a small town environment doesn't appeal to me. I'd like to strike out on my own. I'm afraid my travels in Europe have spoiled me to the good life." He sat quietly as the old white-haired man gazed at him with faded gray eyes. He felt embarrassed for admitting that he really wasn't ready to settle down yet.

"Ah, I see. My son Matthew was of a similar nature. That's my oldest, you know. He had a strong desire to be a coach driver, but I forced him to finish his schooling before taking up the job. He's a fine man, has settled down and married, now that the stages no longer run. Got a passel of young'uns. We get a letter from him occasionally, but don't suppose he'll ever come back into the fold. Doesn't matter. Got plenty of family to keep us busy. Tell you what, young man, you follow your dreams; life's too short to sit around and mildew and fade away. Now, tell me about your pa and ma. What do you hear about the farm? I always longed to see those mountains he wrote about." His eyes sparkled and glowed with an inner fire; and Fuller was forced to reassess the man's character.

Just before they left the room for bed, Baldwin gazed at Fuller thoughtfully and rose. He walked to the shelves, ran a finger across the spines of the books and took one out. He used his shirt sleeve to remove the dust. He crossed over and handed it to Fuller.

"Got a book here for your pa. I think he'd appreciate it more than leaving it to rot until the grandchildren throw it away." A dreamy look came over his face, and Fuller looked at the old leather binding and turned to the frontispiece while Baldwin went back to his seat.

Fuller read the title, *Ivanhoe*, by Sir Walter Scott. The picture was of a man in medieval dress with a steel helmet on his head and riding a horse. He looked up to see Baldwin watching him. Baldwin laughed.

"It's a copy I found in the book store on Jefferson Street; hate to give it up, but these old eyes can't make out the words anymore. You tell Joe I want him to have it."

*****

Fuller heard a sound, and his attention was brought back to his surroundings. The clattering noise and smoke-filled environment of the train encompassed him once again.

An elderly couple were making their slow way down the aisle of the train, his arms loaded with a coat, a basket and a faded carpetbag. The woman was struggling with a shawl draped across her shoulders. The train was slowing for the next stop, and Fuller hoped he had time to stand and stretch his legs. The attendant announced there would be a thirty-minute layover, so Fuller made his way with the other passengers to the stairs and onto the platform.

From this side of the train, he could see only the wall of a massive building and the parking area full of buggies and wagons waiting to take the disembarking passengers to their destinations. The ground near the tracks was littered with trash, and he fleetingly wondered why someone didn't clean it. But, it didn't concern him greatly, for he'd soon be on his way west. He took a cigar and matches from his coat pocket and lit up. He took a deep puff of tobacco, and from somewhere in his past, a memory was conjured up of his grandfather and Standing Tree, the old Arapahoe Indian, sitting under the cottonwood tree smoking. The memory was short-lived but clear. He gazed at the people mingling and talking and saw the elderly couple being greeted by a young man in a blue plaid shirt and overalls, who relieved the man of his burden of baggage. He leaned over to kiss the woman, and Fuller wondered if they were his parents. They turned toward a wagon, and the man in overalls helped the woman into the wagon. Fuller turned away with a frown.

Fuller glanced down the way, his eyes following several passengers he recognized from the train. One couple, younger, had a daughter with them. The girl was wearing a pale green dress with a low, banded waist, white buttons, and white cuffs at the wrists, with black stockings and high-topped brown shoes. She carried a small doll in a dress that matched her own. He'd thought it funny on the train, and it made her stand out to him now. The man in his bowler hat stopped and glanced around, leaning in to whisper to his wife, and she smiled. Then she nodded to a stucco-fronted building with small windows facing the street. Fuller could see the side of the building was of a reddened brick, although he didn't know if it was of local manufacture or not. The man knelt to speak to his daughter, and she pulled her doll up under her arm and ducked her head. His wife shook her head and pulled his arm, and began to move the group inside the building.

Fuller looked more closely, and he could see the signage painted directly on the stucco: Cole Hatfield's Eatery. He laughed. A local dining establishment, and he knew the types of waitresses employed in such places. Young ones, pretty, too, in their trim and tailored outfits. He expected they'd have on caps, too, with curls around their heads. Hungry or not, he intended to see just what was on the menu.

Adjusting his coat, and feeling at his throat to ensure his tie was straight, he dropped his smoke to the sidewalk and ground it under one heel. When a matron walking by frowned at him, sniffling at the blackened scar on the concrete, he laughed. It was a railway stop. She should expect the passengers to leave a mark or two of their presence in the city. Still smiling, he made his way to the stucco building and, holding the door for an elderly man about to exit, he paused and greeted him with, "Afternoon, good sir. I hope you enjoyed your meal."

"Harrumph," was his reply. "Get some decent help, I should say."

"Oh?" Fuller was surprised to hear the man be so churlish. He'd not heard of Hatfield's dining establishment, but it looked clean enough. On the train earlier, he'd asked the conductor about options for purchasing a meal at the next stop, and the man had said nothing indicating problems with the eating arrangements in Abilene. "What makes you say that?"

"Young whippersnappers out to get a man, is what I see. Every one of those women in there will be married in a year, you can bet." The man raised his hand for emphasis, and in his grip was a worn black leather Bible.

"And you are?" Fuller wished to be polite. Who knew but what this man might be important, and he had no wish to offend him. At the same time, he glanced into the establishment. Young women . . . marriage. It didn't sound so bad to him, except for the marriage part.

"Rev. Arthur I. Bledsoe, here to perform a revival. I have a tent already rising out past Potter's Field. Can I expect to see you there, boy?" The man's voice had grown strident, as if he felt the power of God coming over him with the mention of his name.

"I'm just here for a bite to eat." Fuller smiled, but he tried not to make his amusement obvious. "I'm headed to California on the train."

"Ah." Bledsoe's enthusiasm seemed to drain away when he realized Fuller wasn't a possible target for his evangelistic zeal. "I've been to California. Keep watch for my name if I get there again. Bledsoe, Rev. Arthur I. The I is for Ignacio. I share a Spanish heritage from my mother."

"Spanish is fine with me, as long as I can get inside this restaurant before my train leaves." Fuller hoped Bledsoe got the hint.

"Yes, yes, I'll be on my way. A good day to you, young man."

Fuller stepped inside, amused that the gentleman never asked for his name. Inside he found a long counter with an enameled white metal top running down one wall. He selected a seat, pulled his coat and hat off, set them on a second seat and made himself comfortable. Drawing in a deep breath, an unexpectedly pleasing aroma of frying onions assailed him, and he decided he was hungrier than he thought. Meat, he considered, perhaps with green peppers or chili. Steak? He smiled at that. He'd eat a big thick steak, if it tasted as good as it smelled. He picked up a small container with a metal lid and shook a small amount into one hand to discover it was sugar. Perfect for sweetening my drink, he thought, and he brushed it off onto the floor.

"May I help you, sir?'

Fuller looked up to see a smiling young woman at his side, holding a pad of paper and a pencil. He noticed the black and white uniform, and he smiled at her cap perched precariously atop her closely-clipped blonde curls. Her eyes were green with long dark lashes. Her name stitched in black embroidery on her apron read Dolly. She was exactly what he expected.

"I'm on the train—" He barely started when she laughed.

"Oh, I'm sure, sir. Many of our customers are. That also means you want in and out before your train pulls away. You have about twenty minutes, if I'm correct." She glanced up at a clock on the wall, smiling as she did so.

"You know the system, I see, Dolly." Fuller could barely keep his eyes off the collar of her uniform. The top button was undone, exposing her throat, leaving no doubt what a man might find if his fingers were allowed to explore the shadows cast by the overhead lights.

"That I do. I expect you'll want something from our prepared menu. We have chili stew, which is spiced sauce on sausages; roast beef and potatoes, cooked up this very morning; and ham, although it'll be cold, as it's from last night. I'd go with the chili, myself, as I helped prepare it this morning. I know it'll be especially good."

"Do I get a little bit of you with that chili?" Fuller laughed. "If so, you can bring me a double helping."

"You flirt, you." She tapped him on the nose with her pencil. "Can I get you tea or coffee with that?"

"Coffee, please." He reached to her arm, and he chuckled as he drew his hand away. He let his fingertips brush against her hip and slide down her leg.

"Oh, stop it." She giggled, pushing at his hand as she stepped away. "I'll have your lunch here in a half-shake."

Fuller watched her move away, fascinated by her hips as she stepped from foot to foot. Oh, how he wished he wasn't heading out on that train in twenty minutes' time.

By the time she returned, he'd started up a conversation with a slight, middle-aged man wearing a French beret, who didn't remove it as he sat at Fuller's side. It was a soft, flat style of cap, with a button on top, and a small front brim. It was the same brown as his jacket, although his pants contained a woven stripe, and his shoes were of a polished leather. He had a handlebar mustache. Fuller couldn't see his hair, except where it extended past the back of his cap. It was dark and streaked with gray. He began talking of trains, the wheels and boilers, and the amount of power produced by the latest models of steam engines in modern locomotives.

When his chili arrived, Fuller smiled at the waitress, hoping to continue their earlier conversation. She seemed amicable, but the gentleman at his side was insistent to discuss the latest horsepower ratings of the new electrical engines now being constructed in the great dams being built back East. By the time the man pulled a sandwich out of his pocket, unwrapped it carefully and began his own lunch, the waitress was gone, and Fuller was deeply involved in his own meal. The coffee arrived just as Fuller finished up, and he took two sips, laid some coins on the counter to cover his meal, and rushed outside just in time to hear the train whistle blow. Fuller paused just outside the restaurant and lighted a cigar, taking a deep draw, as he observed the couple from earlier already boarding the train. The father now held the doll, and that made Fuller smile. It reminded him of his nephews, and he looked forward to seeing them soon.

The conductor announced the stop over, and Fuller tossed his cigar away. He again took his seat in the passenger car, and was distracted for a moment by the shuffle of feet and the laughter of a child as he ran down the aisle to find a seat, his disgruntled parents following behind. He thought of Dolly's uniform, so trim and crisp, and her walking away from him in the restaurant. As the chug of the wheels jerked him forward, and the screeching whistle blew, warning the buggies and mingling pedestrians to leave the tracks, poor Sally Baldwin never entered his thoughts, except to consider that she didn't hold a candle to beautiful Dolly.

He was thirsty from eating the spicy chili and took out his father's old Army canteen and downed a few swallows. He came to attention when the conductor came down the aisle collecting the tickets of those who had just boarded the train, and Fuller reached out to stop his passage down the aisle.

"How long to Salina?"

"A short time, sir. Do you have your ticket ready?" The conductor smiled, and he held out a clicker he used to mark the passengers' tickets.

"Certainly." Fuller reached into his coat pocket and pulled out a sheaf of papers. He sorted through them, not finding the ticket. "Hold on. I have it somewhere."

"On my way back, sir. I remember you from earlier, so there won't be a problem. Better keep that ticket close by. Next stop's twenty miles away. It's my final one, and the next conductor won't know you."

"Ah, here. Found it!" Fuller had forgotten the extra pocket

sewn in his vest. He now remembered slipping the ticket inside when he removed his coat at the restaurant.

"Thank you, sir, and you have a good ride." With a swift and practiced movement, the man snapped his clicker over the ticket and punched it cleanly. He handed the ticket back to Fuller.

Once again a memory from the past fleeted through Fuller's mind. As a small boy, he'd stood at the door to the high, black stage coach and stamped the tickets of the passengers as they climbed aboard. As clear as a sky blue day in April, he could see the faces of his mother and grandmother waving their handkerchiefs as the coaches drove away and down the road to Denver. His father would pause a moment and go to the corrals to examine the horses for signs of cuts or bruises or harness burn. A feeling of nostalgia struck him as a sharp pain in the gut. He was going home.

The thought was so strange, that he had to swallow the lump in his throat. Not since he'd left the huge ocean liner in New York had he considered the thought of home. To see the green fields, the scattered buildings and the far-distant mountains again seemed like a dream of long ago that he'd forgotten. He'd been gone for over a year on his European tour, seen unbeliev-able sights, tasted exotic foods and smelled the many scents of the Old World; but the fragrant pine and spruce forest of home would always remain with him wherever he went.

And he meant to go far. He'd decided that long ago, when he'd lived in the lonely bondage of the boarding school of his youth. Sent to Maryland at age fourteen to finish his education, he'd spent many nights ashamed to cry, but longing for the forests and mountains of Colorado. He'd been teased unmercifully by the other boys, for his clothes, his speech patterns and his backward manners, but he'd overcome those days with tenacity and skill. He'd attended college and done his internship and residency in a local hospital. He looked down at his black suit, white shirt and silver-colored satin vest. He was dressed to perfection for a doctor and surgeon of his age. He chuckled under his breath. Those callow boys wouldn't laugh at him now; his sophisticated persona wrapped around him like a tight buckskin glove.

He rose and made his way along the aisle to the water closet at the back of the car. The train swayed from side to side, and he grabbed hold of the seat backs to keep from falling. The water closet was primitive at best: a raised pipe in the floor with a seat and a lid. The refuse fell onto the tracks as the train moved along. There were two large bottles of water, some tin cups and clean flannel cloths on a shelf and a receptacle for used paper. A sign on the wall said, "Potable water: Do not waste." He poured some water in a cup and drank, then filled his father's canteen. Closing the door behind him, he had to lean on the wall for balance and slowly made his way to his seat. It was almost full dark, and the attendant went through the car lighting lanterns on the walls. Fuller wrapped himself in his coat and was soon fast asleep, soothed by the rattling of the wheels against the tracks. He awakened several times during the night when the train stopped at other stations.

Two

Fuller could hear the screech of brakes and the wail of the train's horn as it crossed a street and slowed down. They must be arriving at the Denver terminal. His heart began to beat fast as he stood, collected his belongings and picked up the magazines and newspapers he'd read on the road. He'd take them to his father, who loved to read. He thought of the books he'd brought with him, hidden in his bag. He'd found one in a dusty bookstore in London and knew his father would enjoy it. Written in the 18th century, it was about the exploits of William the Conqueror.

A wall of darkness surrounded him as they passed through a tunnel and came to a stop before a sign that read Denver. Ah, he thought, journey's end. And, it had been a long journey, indeed. From the docks at Liverpool in England; the long voyage across the ocean to New York City; by steamboat to Missouri; through the wide plains of Kansas; and finally to his beloved Colorado mountains. He gathered his luggage, his coat and the pile of newspapers and magazines and followed the other passengers out and down the stairs. He went through the turnstile and across the vast open space of the building, and suddenly, there he was.

Fuller's heart flipped when he saw the dear face of his father patiently waiting for him. All the past arguments, disappointments and disagreements disappeared as though they had never been, and he only remembered the love they shared. Fuller crossed the space as though on wings and dropped the whole of his burden, so he could take his father in his arms. He half expected his father to burst out, "Welcome to Sweetwater Station," but the old days were long past, and he felt only the bitter taste of regret that it was so. He drew back.

"Hello, Papa." He looked deeply into his father's eyes and heard a sound behind him. A large man dressed in the clothes of a farmer stood a few feet away. Fuller didn't recognize him.

"Hello, son, did you have a good trip?" Joe Hadley took out his gold-plated timepiece he'd bought with the earnings of catching and training the feral horses of the valleys near their forest home. "You're an hour late." He put the watch back in his pocket and smiled.

Fuller laughed out loud. He picked up his possessions and turned to meet the man who stepped forward with his hand outstretched.

"Name's Tater Stafford, your father's chauffeur and body-guard." He stepped back. "You got some more baggage?'

"Yes, I do. It should be at the baggage counter at the rear of the building under the sign 'H,' I understand. They told us to pick it up there." He started walking beside his father and whispered in his ear, "Chauffeur and bodyguard?"

Joe laughed. "That's just a title for jack-of-all-trades. He's really a farmer, been working in the fields since Monday, planting the garden and hoeing the corn. He's been with us about a year, hails from Tennessee. Your mother's anxious to see you. She said she'd wait for you at home where she belongs. She doesn't fancy the stares and remarks of the people when they see her scarred face for the first time. I told her they don't mean anything by it. But all those years of tending to the cares and whims of the passengers have taken a toll on her good nature." He widened his stride when the huge sign with an "H" written in bold letters was visible a few steps in front of them. Stafford reached it first and told the clerk the name of the man whose luggage they'd come to retrieve.

He turned to Fuller, "How many pieces ya got, sir? You got a ticket?"

Fuller dropped his bag, gave his coat to his father to hold and searched his pockets for the ticket stub that identified his luggage. He handed it to Stafford and waited for the clerk to unscramble the lot of bags, boxes, and crates being brought from the bowels of the train's baggage compartment. It took a while for it all to be located, and they found a small cart and piled it high.

He reached in his pocket and gave the attendant a coin, saying, "Thanks." The attendant nodded and moved to the next passenger.

Before Fuller could say anything more, he found himself outside on the grassy parking area in front of a faded-black, dusty surrey. Behind the vehicle stood a flatbed wagon, and a short, stubby man of middle age began to lift the baggage piece by piece onto the wagon bed. Fuller was struck by the strength of the man. The weight of the boxes seemed to be nothing to him. He looked at him more closely.

"Papa?" he whispered to his father.

"Name's Elmer Hagar; he's been here about a year, runs the saw mill." When the man had the luggage on the wagon and tied with a heavy cord, he turned, and Joe introduced him.

"Elmer, this is my oldest son, Fuller, just back from Europe." Joe couldn't keep the pride from his voice.

"Pleased to meet you, sir." Hagar stepped forward to shake hands and withdrew to mount the seat of the wagon. As he stepped up, Fuller could see a patch on the sleeve of his coat and a larger one on the tail near the hem. It was neat and of a lighter color than the material of the coat.

"Best get aboard, son. It's a long way to Sweetwater. The ladies will have a meal ready when we get there." Joe climbed aboard the surrey and looked to see Hagar patiently holding the reins to the wagon. He raised his voice, "We'll go ahead Elmer, so we don't have to breathe the dust. You come along behind."

Stafford had the craggy, rough skin of a man who spent hours in the sun; and he sported broad shoulders and slender hips, long legs, and hair worn longer than was fashionable. Fuller supposed that he had no time to visit a barber, and maybe Hannah or his wife cut his hair. Joe hadn't said, nor had Fuller asked if the man was married. He supposed he'd find out everything when he arrived at the farm among the pine forest. He took a deep breath and climbed into the back seat.

Stafford drove, and Joe sat in the front passenger seat. The drone of the horse's hooves and the smack of the wheels on the dirt road soon took their toll, and Fuller drifted off to sleep, his chin falling on his chest. He awoke with a jerk a few times and looked around him, conscious of his environment, but too comfortable to engage the other men in conversation. The wind blew across his face, and he took off his hat, so it didn't fall off his head and onto the road. A few times as they rounded a sharp curve or hit a bump, he grabbed the medical bag at his side to keep it from being tossed onto the floor. At last he saw the first of the giant Ponderosa pines, the junipers and the majestic spruce; and he knew he was nearing his home. He smelled the scent of flowers and clear air, with a touch of overheated horseflesh as they moved along. He smiled and leaned forward.

"Papa, do you smell it?" He placed a hand on his father's shoulder and glanced at Stafford, who'd heard him and turned his head in speculation.

"Yes, son. I've been smelling that same smell for nigh on twenty-six years now. See the mountains? They still have snow from the winter storms. I don't reckon you saw no mountains as pretty as those on your trip overseas, did you?" Joe turned his head back around, and Fuller laughed. He'd seen some tall mountains and some deep valleys; and the ocean waves and the slums of Europe; but to his father, these mountains and valleys would always be superior, he supposed. He was happy that it was so, but the dream of his last few months began to nag at his mind. He knew his papa would want him to settle down at the farm, or maybe in Denver or somewhere nearby and start a medical practice, but he wasn't ready. It put a damper on his spirits, and he spent the rest of the trip in deep thought.

Three

As though the dreams of his future were lost in the scenes of the past, Fuller raised his head and saw the tall trees pass swiftly by. He felt the dark secrets of the forest as they rode the last mile and came out into the open meadow wherein stood the buildings, the corrals and the sheds of the former relay stage station for the Overland Stage and Mail Service. Memories came crashing in on him, and he gazed in awe at the sight. He wondered what his father was thinking and couldn't imagine the past as it was once lived. The surrey passed the original house and came to a stop near the large white two-story structure of his adulthood. It had been over a year since he'd been home, and nothing seemed to be different but him. He'd changed, matured and gained knowledge of the world, but the small farm in Colorado had always been here, waiting, just as he knew his mother and his grandmother, Ruth, were waiting.

When the wagon came to a total stop, a young boy came running from the corrals and stood, open-mouthed and silent, as Stafford climbed out. He circled the front of the conveyance and stood respectfully as Joe and Fuller stepped down. Fuller felt his heart race, and his hands grew damp as he looked around him. His eyes automatically took in the sights, and he gazed at the slight rise above the spring, to the mounds of the people who had lived and died here; he turned to see the weathered, brownish-gray walls of his birthplace and the huge brick barn built by his father, Buck Jones and his Apache wife, Rosie, and Jeremiah Fuller. He was familiar with the tales of the past, and he took it all in as he breathed the scent of pine, wood smoke and meat cooking as it drifted away into the air.

"Well, son, what do you think? You ready to greet your mother and grandmother? This young man is your sister's boy, Franklin. There's another one like him in the house. Come along, now. No need in keeping the ladies waiting longer. Tater, you take the baggage in the house and just leave it in the hallway. I know you're anxious to get to that mare in the barn. I'll see you later, when the excitement settles down. Thanks for the ride into Denver. It seems to get longer every year; guess it's these old bones of mine." He laughed and started walking with vigor to the white house.

The wide door opened, and Fuller could see the women step through and stand on the porch waiting for him. He took off at a run, jumped the steps without feeling the soles of his shoes touch the wood and opened his arms. Hannah Hadley, the scar on her face still clearly visible, wrapped her arms around her first-born son and began to cry.

He hugged her tight, then withdrew, and without a word, drew his grandmother into his arms. He whispered, "I love you," into her ear and turned to the third woman, standing with a small boy at her skirts. "Janey?" She, too, was given a hug and released, and he turned to the boy. "Hello, young Mark, and how are you?" The boy drew back and tried to hide behind his mother. Fuller laughed and ruffled his hair. He stood, all of them wanting to say something, but none wanting to be the first to say it. He was rescued by Joe, who mounted the steps and handed his wife a snow white handkerchief.

"Come, Hannah, darling, I'm hungry enough to eat a mule, hide, hooves and all. The boy's home where he belongs, and it's time for dinner." He turned to Tater Stafford. "You're welcome to eat with us tonight, if you've a notion to."

"Thanks, Joe, but we'll let you have the first night with your family. But, I'll expect a piece of Hannah's apple pie tomorrow when the dust settles. I'll call you to let you know if the foal has arrived."

Joe took his wife's arm and ushered her and Ruth into the house. Janey fell in line, and Fuller took one more quick look at the distant mountains covered in snow and followed, holding the door for Franklin to pass in front of him. He gazed with surprise at the banner strung across the upper hallway from wall to wall. "Welcome home, Fuller." He swallowed hard, knowing he'd soon leave again, because he must follow his heart, which drew him away.

"Ah, who did this? Janey, was this your idea?"

She laughed and cuffed him on the arm. Four years younger than her brother, she'd married Walter Abernathy, the son of the animal handler Roland Abernathy, who had remained at the farm when his father died. Called Bub by the family, they lived in the original house built by the stage company carpenters in 1866, when Joe and Hannah had first arrived at Sweetwater Springs.

Stafford and his wife lived in the log cabin that Joe had built for his parents, which the wheelwright had used for his shop and forge when the brown coach had been robbed and wrecked by bandits on the road. The driver Paul Ward had survived and moved on to the west to drive a stage in another state. The shotgun messenger, Manning, and three passengers had been killed.

"Has anyone heard from that brother of mine?" Fuller had considered stopping by the Army post at Fort Riley in Kansas to see his brother, but he hadn't been certain that Johnie was there.

Hannah said with a frown, "We haven't heard from Johnie in months; I worry about him and pray for his safety."

"Now, darling," Joe consoled. "No need to worry over the boy; he's probably gone on patrol, and there's no mail delivery."

"Right, Mama." Fuller leaned in and gave her a kiss on the forehead, and he laughed. "He must be able to take care of himself by now, joining the Army at eighteen." In spite of his comment, Fuller didn't know Johnie well, for he'd left home himself at an early age for boarding school, medical university and the more recent year in Europe, while the boy was growing to adulthood.

Janey patted her mother's arm, saying, "You have me, Mama. I'll never leave you." Together they led the others into the kitchen.

Fuller followed them and was surprised when a woman with

short blonde curls turned from the stove. He didn't remember ever seeing a more beautiful, full-figured woman in all his travels. She smiled, and his heart beat faster.

"Fuller, honey, this is Tater's wife, Winifred. We call her Winnie; she's a jewel of great value. She's cooked most of the meal today to give us time to spruce up and get ready for your arrival. Winnie, love, this is my oldest son, James Fuller Hadley, come home at last." Winnie dropped the spoon she was holding and walked forward with a smile on her face to shake hands.

Fuller struggled hard to hold his disappointment in check. She was married, and to the hired hand, his mind said, as he took her small hand in his hand. He smiled and muttered some kind of greeting that must have satisfied everyone, for they all began to take a place at the table. To distract his thoughts, he gazed up at the opposite wall and gulped. There, hanging in the place of honor, was a watercolor painting of Standing Tree, the Arapahoe Indian who had wandered onto the station grounds during a storm. His mother had painted the portrait, and it was a good likeness, his blanket wrapped around his shoulders, and his black eyes open with a sense of awareness of the future. Beside the painting, hanging on pegs, were his bow and quiver and the medicine bag that hung around his neck. Fuller was stunned. He was young when Standing Tree had died during a mustang hunt, but he could remember as clear as day the tall Indian holding him in his arms and comforting him.

Fuller looked at his father and saw the admiration and respect he still had in his heart for his Indian friend. "Papa?" His father turned and looked first at Hannah, and then at Fuller.

"It was your mother's idea. She said there was no sense in putting the things in the attic where no one would see them. She painted the picture from memory, and a damn good job it is. Now, let's eat. Janey, where's your husband? He should be here."

"He's at the saw mill, Papa. I'll give him a call." She left the room to use the telephone, and everyone sat down, except Hannah and Winnie. Hannah brought the bread to the table and placed it before Fuller. Winnie brought a bowl in each hand: one containing mustard greens and one with boiled potatoes. Soon, a large roast beef and carrots, onions, pickles, spiced beets and large platter with corn on the cob dripping with butter were on the table, and last came a huge coffee pot. A pitcher of milk was there for those who drank milk.

Walter came in and shook hands with Fuller. He looked older, Fuller thought. His hair had streaks of gray, and he'd gained weight, but it was the same Bub with whom he'd hidden in the hay stacks and swam in the spring. They smiled at each other and took their places at the table.

"Welcome home, Fuller, it's been a long time. How did you like the sea voyage?"

The conversation drifted from the home-coming to the weather, to the farm happenings, to the children's schooling and to the country's politics. And finally, when Fuller was sated and drew back, he decided he may as well make his big announcement while everyone was together.

"Papa, Mama, Granny Ruth, I want to say something." Everyone looked up and gazed at him in amazement. He'd never been one to speak up at the table before, always letting the others speak while he ate.

"Papa, I know you'll be unhappy with my decision, but I'm not staying here long." He heard a gasp from his mother, and a spoon fell from Walter's hand. He looked around at his family and back to his father, who sat with a sad but resigned look on his face.

"Go on, son. What are your plans?"

"As you all know, of course, I'm a doctor, fully trained and with the paper to prove it. I've been in some of the capitals of the world, seen mighty rivers and the ruins and tombs of ancient people. I've seen some of the richest and most valued paintings done by the masters of Europe and Italy; and I've also seen some slums where people beg and steal for their food. This spot will always have a special place in my heart, but I can't live here. I plan to go to San Francisco and start a practice with a fellow I met at university. He's already bought a large house in which we'll have our surgery and office and our living quarters in the back. We plan to minister to the ill and the downhearted. Of course, we'll probably have to have a few wealthy patients to help with expenses, but mostly we'll work with those who can't afford to pay for our service." He stopped talking and looked first at his father, then his mother, and waited for their reaction.

"But, son, there are poor people living here in Colorado. Why do you have to go to California to find them? There's slums in Denver, and you'd be close to home." Joe was trying in his common sense way to understand this shocking news.

Hannah kept her eyes on the table, tears forming in her eyes, but she blinked them away.

"You're being selfish, just like you've always been. Selfish and cruel. Papa and Mama have sacrificed and worked hard their whole lives, and you haven't done one thing to repay them. I'm the one, and Walter, who've had to keep up the farm and do the manual labor, while you trek over Europe and see those fancy paintings and things you said. When will it be our turn to see the world? We don't even get a week to see the opera or the museums in Denver." Janey was crying in earnest, and Walter put his arm around her, a shocked look on his face.

"Now, Janey, girl. You hush. Your mother and I know what you've done for us, and we thank you, but you don't remember the old days when we first came here to live. Hannah, do you remember how it was, when there was no road through the forest, and no barn or sheds or comforts like we have today?" Joe looked around at the table and the dishes and glassware. His eyes drifted as if by design to the bow and quiver of arrows and the painting of Standing Tree.

"Fuller, we'll need to talk about this some more. Tonight is for celebrating your homecoming. If everyone's finished, we'll help with the cleaning up so Winnie can get home to her house, and we'll talk of other things." He started to pick up a plate and was stopped by Hannah's voice.

"Joe, I have something to say." Everyone looked at Hannah. "It's true, Joe and I came to this place when we were young and frightened and inexperienced. You young ones can't imagine the way it was, all alone, the two of us, with the responsibilities of the animals and the coaches, and the drivers and the farm. Look around you, Fuller, and you, Janey, and see what we've built. Joe worked, sometimes day and night, to build the barn and the other buildings to make a home for us. When the rumors started that the railroad was coming and the stage lines would shut down, we made the decision to buy the land and the forest, and the spring that feeds the creek. It was a great challenge, a sometimes lonely life, for the whole station and the coaches and drivers depended on us. Now, you say, Fuller, that you want to live in far-away California and work with the poor people. Janey, you think that makes him selfish and uncaring of his family. But, it's not true. Joe and I appreciate every day your love and concern for us. Mama, do you remember how it was when the war was over?" She paused and looked at Ruth, who nodded and smiled, a sad smile, for she had lost a son, James, in the war, and had lost her oldest son, Luther, in a barn fire in Indiana.

"I grew up in my uncle's home, where I was mistreated and abused, not only because of my face, but because my parents died in the fire that scarred my face. I praise God for the day that Joe came and asked for my hand in marriage, but I was frightened, too, because I'd never been farther than a few miles from my home." She smiled, took Joe's hand in hers and patted it. "Joe and I've known each other all our lives; for all that I'm two years older than him. We went to the same church services, until my aunt decided she didn't like the preacher. We rode the steamboats and the stage coach to get here; it took us weeks of hard travel. But, we came, and it's our home. Now, Fuller, you go to California, if you think that's where you'll be happy and can help other people to heal and best serve in your practice. Joe, do you remember Slim, and how he took care of Paul when the coach was robbed? Do you remember how he took the thorn from Standing Tree's leg when it festered and caused the fever?"

"Yes, I remember." Joe smiled at her, and she smiled back.

Fuller watched in amazement at this bond that they shared between them. Would he ever find such love and satisfaction with someone? He looked at his grandmother and knew that she and Grandpa had shared the same love and harmony. He glanced down at his empty plate and remembered the cracked plates and crockery of his youth. He rose and went to his mother and gave her a kiss on her scarred face, as he had seen his father do in his youth. "Thank you, Mama."

As though of one accord, they each rose and helped clear the table; Winnie left for her home, and Janey and Hannah cleaned the dishes and put away the leftover food. The children were put to bed. Joe, Fuller and Walter went into the parlor and discussed the trip to California and the practice of medicine in a large city. They talked of the farm, and Fuller knew that Walter and the hired hand, Stafford, would see that his father and mother and grandmother were fed and cared for. For the first time in months, he felt at peace as he wished them all goodnight and mounted the stairs to the guest room in the large white house. He blew out the lamp and gazed out the window at the mountain peaks against an unruly charcoal sky, barely seen in the darkness over the tops of the trees. Clouds had begun to darken the horizon. Even the stars were being eaten by the expanding blackness, and he wondered whether the violent weather he remembered from his youth would crash across the landscape before the sun rose to wipe it all away in the morning. He turned from the window and smiled, thinking of the courage and daring of his mother; the tenacity and strength of his father; and the unconditional love of his grandmother. Janey, he wasn't so sure of, but he was pleased that he had Walter on his side. He climbed into the strange bed and fell asleep.

That night, the storm did roll in. The wind whistled around window frames in the big, white house, rattling the occasional loose pane that suffered from lack of calk. A venting mechanism in the kitchen wall clattered with each fist of wind, and the house popped and groaned with the onset of the rain. Sheets of water beat against the walls, trying to work their way inside, but the house was well built.

The hail pounding on the roof awoke Fuller from a sound sleep. It was a sound he hadn't heard for years. He remembered how frightened the travelers on the stages had been when the storms rolled in. They'd hunker down in front of the station fireplace with the shutters pulled tight and several lamps burning brightly to beat back the darkness. Joe would bring out board games and old magazines provided by the stage line to entertain them. One of his earliest memories was of such a night, sitting in his grandfather's lap being read to from a book. They could only guess at the damage being done outside until the shutters were released from their catches, as there had been no windows to see through. It was a good memory for Fuller, reminding him of a part of his childhood that had changed little in nearly twenty years.

*****

Joe and Hannah lay in each other's arms and talked for a

long time, their window dark, and the curtains firmly closed. They remembered chicken coops turned over, roofs ripped off and work to be done after the storms of previous years passed by. There was nothing to be done in the middle of the night, however, and they were secure in their bed.

*****

Janey and Walter had an argument, and in the disagreement, very vocal and very long, the storm seemed a muted background appropriate to their rising anger. It built, battered against what it couldn't blast out of the way, and then relented, leaving the Sweetwater farm as it had been all along, firmly rooted in the soil of Colorado. The storm began to wane, and finally Janey settled for what she couldn't change, for she'd always known that Fuller wouldn't be happy on the farm. In the end, as the final storm clouds cleared from the sky, she drew her arms around her husband and held him tight, secure in his love and strength. She drifted off to sleep in the bedroom that had once been her parents' in the weathered stage relay station house where she was born.

Four

Early the next morning, before the sun had grown hot and yellow in the sky, Fuller Hadley dressed and went outside. The ground under the trees was wet with the storm from the night before. He breathed in the clean, mountain air, and from old habit strolled around the perimeter of the farm, watching for critters or fallen logs from the split rail fence. He walked to the spring and waved his hand through the ice cold water, scooped up a handful and drank it. He gazed at the mountains and moved on to the graveyard among the trees. He knew exactly where to look and stood at the rock-covered mound of his stillborn sister, Anne, who died when he was about two years old. There were some wilted flowers on the stones, and he knew his mother had brought them there. He went to the grave of his grandfather, took off his hat, and knelt at the stone carved with his name; next he went to the grave of Jeremiah Fuller, for whom he was named. There he found the weathered boulder with the hand-carved date and his name. He paused for a moment, rubbed the surface indentations of the date, thinking of that day and the sacrifice the young man had made for his father. He moved on to the graves of Standing Tree, Roland Abernathy, Dakota and Brody White, and two mounds of people he didn't know. He supposed they'd been workers on the stage station or more recently on the farm. He looked toward the spring and saw his father moving around the corrals.

He left the graveyard and walked to his father's side. "Good morning, Papa. Did you sleep well?"

Joe Hadley smiled. "Slept well enough. I was thinking about what you said and decided you'd need some spending money for your expenses." He reached in his pocket and took out a roll of bills. He put it in Fuller's hand. "Now, don't tell your mama I gave it to you. She'll probably slip you some of her own household account. She'll think it's a big secret. So, I won't say a word more. Come see the new horse I bred from one of Mack's descendants." He stretched out his steps, taking long strides, and Fuller had a hard time keeping up with him. "He's about six months old; still a young'un, but has potential as a breeder. Has some of the wild mustang in him. I call him Tenacity. Hannah says that's a foolish thing to call a horse, but I call him that anyway." He opened the barn door and lit the lantern hanging on the peg. He raised it above his head and led Fuller to the stall.

"Gonna get electricity in here one of these days. Tater says he can do it, if he has the wiring, but I've put it off. Well, here he is." He opened the door of the stall and the horse came to him. Joe held out his hand with a piece of apple for the colt. Fuller scratched between his ears, and without conscious thought, examined him as his father had taught him when he was young.

Joe moved on to the next stall. As he opened the door, Fuller could see that a mare was on the ground, moaning. He watched as Joe tried to get the mare on her feet. The horse rose and stood on wobbly legs. He ran his hand slowly over her belly and down her legs, speaking in a soft, gentle voice. He reached in a bucket for some grain, but the horse backed away and tossed her head.

"What's wrong, Papa?" Fuller stayed near the entrance, holding the lantern high, and remained still, so as not to frighten the mare.

Joe turned and withdrew from the stall, clicking the door shut behind him. "The old gal's not been eating right. Tater says if we don't get some grain down her, we may lose the foal." He stopped abruptly. "Or, we might lose the mare. Name's Candy. Janey said her color coating looks like taffy. She's a gentle soul; the boys ride her when she's not in this condition." He walked to the entrance of the barn, waited while Fuller blew out the lantern and hung it on its peg.

Fuller helped pull the barn door shut and followed Joe. He could hear the pride and appreciation in his father's voice for each of the horses born and raised on the farm. From the barn they moved to the house. As they came to the steps, Fuller could smell bacon frying and coffee brewing. He stopped on the porch and looked toward the old house; Walter was mending a broken shutter damaged by the wind or hail. He entered the house and almost bumped into this father, who had stopped to put his hat on the peg. He decided old habits died hard, for there was a row of pegs for hats and coats on the wall beside the door. And a tall, round tin for umbrellas sat on the floor.

They moved to the kitchen where Hannah was stirring porridge in a pot. She turned as though instinctively feeling the presence of her mate.

"Morning, honey. Did you show Fuller the new colt?" She put her spoon on the table, grabbed a cloth and removed a flat, square pan full of fluffy, brown biscuits from the oven. "Fuller, sit down, and I'll pour you some coffee." She paused, an odd look on her face. "Do you drink coffee?"

"Yes, Mama, I do. Thanks. Those biscuits smell good. I was hoping you'd bake some of your sweet rolls this morning. The taste of your sweet rolls has haunted me for months. Couldn't wait to get home for them." He looked at his father, who was laughing at him.

"I'll bake some tomorrow." She poured coffee for both men and turned back to bring the pot of porridge to the table. She brought a platter of bacon and placed it in front of Joe, and he took a slice and put it in his mouth. "Did he tell you he named that colt Tenacity? I don't know much about breeding horses, but I hope that animal lives up to his fancy name." She poured herself a cup of coffee and sat down to eat.

"Tell me about this friend of yours that you'll work with in California," she said between bites. And, without thinking, Fuller was telling them about his dreams and plans. He was grateful it was just them this morning. When they'd finished eating, Joe rose to go outside, but Fuller stayed in the house. He wandered into the parlor, where he saw the curio cabinet standing in a corner.

He took a small glass figurine from the shelf and admired

the craftsmanship. He noticed there were a few that he didn't recognize and thought to ask his mother about them. He fingered one of the tiny Napoleon soldiers of his childhood, but his eyes were caught by the walnut case that held his great-grandfather's dueling pistols and took it from the shelf. He laid the case on the table near the fireplace and raised the lid. He wondered if they still smelled of gun powder, but they didn't. There was a faint smell of oil, and he assumed that his father took them out and oiled them occasionally, but he put them away on the shelf and went to the dining room to look at Standing Tree's bow and arrows and the medicine bag.

He reached his hand out and gently touched the colorful beads. He jumped when his father spoke behind him. He withdrew his hand as though he were a small guilty boy, caught in mischief.

"Do you want to take it with you? It's yours, you know. Standing Tree gave it to me for you." Joe reached for the pouch and took it from the peg. He held it reverently in his hand. "I remember as though it were yesterday, the day he went with me into the forest and told me the story of his family. Do you remember?" He took the pouch and sat on the sofa near the fireplace.

"Yes, Papa, but I'd like to hear it again, please." He pulled a chair near Joe's knees and sat down.

Joe smiled. He twisted the rough rawhide strap around his finger. "His grandfather's name was Lone Deer. He lived somewhere near Fort Laramie; I don't know exactly where; maybe he lived somewhere else. I just know the tribe was living there when Standing Tree found us. He said his father was Wolf

Killer, and I thought at the time that was funny, for Standing Tree and Buck Jones, my first animal handler, went off one day without asking for permission and tracked some wolves and killed them. It was soon after that when Buck left with his Conestoga and two of the stage horses. But, that's a different story. Standing Tree said he had a wife named Face in the Moon and a boy child; but he didn't tell me the name of the child. He said when he was a small boy, like Franklin, his grandfather told him about his dream that Standing Tree would one day live with the white men. But, the boy didn't believe him, and his father was killed in a battle with the Crow. So, he was raised at a mission in Arkansas where they taught him our language and other things, but he hated the white men, because they brought the fever to the Indians. I suppose cholera, scarlet fever or measles, I don't know; but his wife and child died, and he went hunting for white men to kill and forgot his grandfather's dream until he was an old man. Standing Tree said that he had no family, no sons and no wife, no one to cook for him; so the elders of the tribe sent him away." He looked up to see Hannah had come quietly into the room and sat down.

"We had a terrible hail storm. The barn wasn't built yet, and we had to provide a shelter for the animals. Do you remember, Hannah?"

"I remember, Joe, go on. What did Standing Tree tell you?"

"He said he hid in a cave waiting to die; but he didn't die. When the rain and hail stopped, he started walking. He was hungry and tired, and he saw the smoke from the chimney and laid down beside the wall, covered in that old smelly blanket he wore that day. Near dawn Hannah went to the outhouse, and he woke up and saw her, but he pretended to be asleep, because he was frightened that we'd kill him. He said again he waited to die; but he didn't die." Joe laughed as he thumbed the beads on the pouch.

"He said he saw me come out with my long gun in my hands, and again he waited to die, but instead I fed him some bacon and part of your mother's pie. I told Buck to make him take a bath. He smelled bad, and I was afraid of lice or vermin in his hair or on his body. It was Rosie who interpreted for us. Buck knew a few Apache words and sign language, but Rosie talked to Standing Tree." He stopped as though remembering, and the other two kept quiet. "I was nervous, but Hannah wasn't. She acted as though we had Indians drop in on us for breakfast every day. When Buck made him bathe and wash his hair, I gave him some of my clothes and a clean blanket. He came in the house and sat at the table like stone. He didn't like coffee; we found that out right away. But, he sure liked to smoke. Your grandfather gave him a cigar, and eventually he learned how to strike a match and light his own smokes. When the new supply caravan came through, there were some pipes and tobacco, and he preferred that method of smoking." Again Joe stopped as he saw Franklin come in with Janey and Mark, and they took seats.

"Well, that's about the story. He took up permanent residence with us. He told me that day in the forest to keep this bag until you were grown and tell you of Lone Deer, his grandfather, of Wolf Killer, his father, of Face in the Moon, his wife, and the days before the Arapahoe died of the fever. He said to tell you of the Dream that Came True, old Lone Deer's dream from Father in the Sky that someday Standing Tree would make his home with the white man."

"No, Papa, you keep the bag, and give it to my son, someday, if I ever have one; or to one of these boys, so the legend will go on for generations. I wish I could've had more time with him. I just remember him holding me tight in his arms; and when he sat at the table; and when we went on that last mustang hunt and he died. What's in the bag; did he show you?" Fuller could feel his heart beating steadily and was aware of the curiosity of the boys. He knew that if Joe didn't show them, they would open it sometime when alone to see for themselves.

"Nothing much." He opened the bag and took out a root, a feather and a turquoise stone. "He said they represent the earth, the sky and the water, the basic elements of life. See, boys? Just ordinary things, nothing to get excited about. But, to him they meant a lot." He let the boys feel and examine the items, and he put them back in the bag and hung it on its peg. "Would you fellows like to hold the bow and arrows?"

"Yes," they replied in unison. Joe took them carefully from the wall and let the boys try their hand at shooting an arrow, but they weren't strong enough to open the bow to its widest point. He let them feel the sharp point of the arrows and hung them back on the wall. He turned to them.

"Boys, I want you to promise me faithfully not to touch the Indian's possessions again until you're given permission by your parents or until you're grown up. Will you promise me?" When Joe had that piercing glare in his eyes, even Fuller felt he needed to promise. Janey rose, and to lighten the atmosphere, she led her boys out of the room. Hannah followed her into the kitchen.

"Thanks, Papa. I'm glad to know that Standing Tree had a good life here at the station." He glanced again at the portrait and knew why Hannah had asked it to be hung there.

"Come with me, son. Let's saddle some horses and ride. I need some exercise." Fuller was glad to agree, and they went to the barn, saddled a couple of horses and rode to the boundaries of the property. Joe pointed out things he wanted his son to know. They rode to the saw mill, dismounted and watched the workers for an hour and rode back to the house. Fuller was sore, for it had been years since he'd ridden a horse. He helped Joe unsaddle the horses, and while Joe checked on the mare, he walked down to the old stage coach station house and did some exploring. He came across Winnie hanging out the wash, and his heart beat faster. She was so beautiful, but she was married.

The days passed swiftly, and when Fuller began to have night sweats and wake up with his thoughts on Winnie's breasts, he knew it was time to leave. He told his parents at supper on a Wednesday when he'd been there two weeks that he had reservations on the train bound for California. He was surprised when his mother cornered him and gave him a small velvet bag. He thought of what his father had said and expected to see some money, but it was a wide, gold wedding band.

"It was my mother's ring. I didn't know her because I was very small when the house fire injured my face and killed my folks. I want you to have it. You'll find someone that you can love. Give it to her. If she doesn't like it, then send it back, and I'll give it to Janey or Johnie for his wife." She sighed. "It may be that Johnie'll never marry. He wanted to join the Army, and

I told Joe he was too young, but he was determined. I miss him."
She smiled. "I'll miss you, too. Write to me when you can."

"I promise, Mama, I'll write. Don't worry about me. I'm a doctor. I know how to take care of myself." He gave her a hug.

Later, he was reading the newspaper in the parlor, when his grandmother poked her head in to see if he was alone. When she saw that he was, she crossed the room and stood wringing her hands, taking furtive glances at the door.

"Yes, Grandmother, did you want to tell me something?"

She took one more look at the door and put her hand in the pocket of her apron, drew it out and handed him a package wrapped in brown paper. "Here's some spending money. A man never has enough. Now, don't tell me you don't want it; 'cause I'll never have a place to spend it. The money sits in the bank and grows dust; you use it for some poor family who needs it. Your grandfather would be proud of you." She hugged him and made her way from the room before he could say anything.

He unwrapped the paper gift and saw inside a twenty-dollar gold piece. He gasped and sighed. Very generous, very generous indeed. He wondered if Janey would slip him some money, too. But, it was Bub who drew him aside a few minutes before Tater was to drive him to the train terminal.

"Now, I've known you since we were boys together and the stages ran regularly, and I admire your spunk and tenacity. I'm happy to stay here and work the farm for your father, so Janey and I don't need much. I want you to take this money and buy food for those starving children you were telling us about. Maybe the good Lord will give me a gold star instead of those silvery ones we see every night in the sky above the mountains.

47

You take care of yourself and don't get into trouble with the law." Walter handed him a small leather pouch.

The next morning, the family watched as Fuller left the Sweetwater Creek for the long, slow ride across the mountains and plains of the western United States. He gave the women and children hugs, shook hands with his father and Walter, and slipped into the passenger seat beside Tater Stafford, who was driving him to the terminal. He sighed and settled down in the seat so he could better see the tops of the Ponderosas and the junipers and the spruce as they passed by. He breathed the scent of his home, knowing that it was possible that he would never return, but he wouldn't dwell on that possibility. He turned his head to see the hired hand driving the flatbed wagon with his luggage. There was a trail of dust behind them.

After a few minutes, he raised himself to a sitting position, and they began to talk. Fuller asked about the farm, and Tater responded with enthusiasm. From the talk of horses and future garden crops, they moved to other things, and Fuller learned how the man received his name.

It seemed that there was a very hard drought in Tennessee when he was a boy, and there were six children in his family. The vegetables that grew above the ground like peanuts, corn and grain wilted and died. His father considered selling his prize bull for seed to replant, but a neighbor sold him a couple bushels of potatoes instead. The root vegetables stayed firm and good. His mother sent him and his older sister and two younger brothers to school with boiled cold potatoes for their dinner. The other children went home to eat if they lived nearby, or brought biscuits and sausage or ham. One of the older boys started calling him 'Tater, to mock him. Stafford challenged him to a fist fight after school. He laughed as he remembered the fight.

"I whupped him bad. He came to school the next day with a tooth missing and black eyes. But, the name stuck; I've been called Tater ever since. Even my pa and ma called me Tater before they died."

"What about the bully? What happened to him?"

"Oh, we became best friends. He's a lawyer and married to my sister, Mariah."

"Why'd you come to Colorado?"

"I came to work on the railroad. Jobs was scarce and with all those children, someone had to get out of the house, so's the others had enough to eat."

"How many children are there?"

"Eleven."

"You have ten brother and sisters?"

"Yep, more than that if'n you count the in-laws; last I took note there's about fifty in the family now, counting the nieces and nephews. I get letters from them and write them back. I'd sure like to go back to see 'em someday. But, I never seem to have the time. Winnie says we can go after the baby comes, but I don't know. Seems then we'll have a start on our own eleven and never get back home. I 'preciate the way you done come right out and told your family how you was wanting to go to California. That must have been hard." He glanced at Fuller and back to the road.

Fuller didn't know what to say, so he reached for the one fact that bothered him. "You're going to have a child soon?"

"Sure am; maybe in the fall, Winnie said. I'm proud as can be; I want five or six, but she says we have to wait and see. Can't rush these things."

Fuller didn't respond. Tater seemed to be engrossed in his own thoughts, and they arrived at the train station in plenty of time to eat a meal and check his baggage. He kept only his bulging doctor's satchel, a small valise and his heavy coat with him, in case he got cold in the night. They parted with a handshake, and Tater and the hired man left for the long drive back to Sweetwater Springs. Fuller felt forlorn, for now he had no one with whom to talk. He saw on older gentleman who seemed alone, and they struck up a conversation, but it was short lived, for the man was in the coach section and Fuller in First Class. He sat and watched the scenery out his window until the sun set and he was in the dark with only a dim light in the train car. When he caught himself again thinking of Winnie Stafford's breasts, he decided to take a few days to explore the city before he contacted his friend.

Five

Fuller arrived at the train terminal in Oakland on a Tuesday morning and checked into a hotel with a comfortable bed and a water closet down the hallway. He arose on a Friday, ate breakfast at a clean, but shabby restaurant and spent an hour at the tonsorial parlor, where he had a steaming warm bath, his hair cut, his fingernails neatly trimmed and his shoes shined. Only he and the night clerk knew of the interval in which he spent a most pleasant time with a full-figured woman named Marigold with flaming red hair and a mole on her chin. Feeling appeased and consoled, Fuller rode the ferry across the bay to San Francisco. He called at the address he'd been given by his friend, Doctor Edward Murray.

The door knocker was answered by a middle-aged woman with a frown on her face and her gray hair fashioned securely on top of her head with hairpins and tortoise shell combs. A single strand had escaped to hang loosely at her left ear. She pulled it back and sighed.

"Yes, sir? What may I do for you? The doctor doesn't see patients until the afternoon. If it's an emergency, you'd best go to the St. Michael's Hospital on Cedar Hill Lane." She started to close the door, but Fuller smiled in his most charming manner, and she melted on the spot.

"Ma'am, I'm Doctor Fuller Hadley, your new employer, perhaps?" He heard a sound behind the woman, and a brown-haired man with green eyes grinned at Fuller. He was of medium height and build and dressed in sober black. He stepped around Mrs. Frances Bolade, and held out his hand.

"Fuller, I'm so glad you finally came. I feel like I've been swept down a river without a canoe. Come in. Come in. Mrs. Bolade, if you please, this is my partner, Fuller Hadley. He'll be wanting to go to his room and put away his luggage. How did you come?" He looked out the door and saw a wagon pulled by two horses and driven by a portly man dressed in a dark coat and felt hat. Seeing the conveyance, he shuttled Fuller and Mrs. Bolade aside and moved down the steps toward the wagon.

Fuller looked at Mrs. Bolade and grinned. "Pleased to meet you, ma'am." He tipped his hat and turned aside to watch his friend at the wagon. The driver tied the reins of his team to the horse stop and descended to help heave the luggage onto the sidewalk.

With a sigh, Fanny Bolade explained that she was preparing soup for her employer's dinner, and it mustn't be left unattended for long. Fuller followed her. She stooped to glance at a cake in the oven, opened the door and saw that it was done, pulled it from the hot orifice and placed it on a rack on the table, then limped up the stairs to make sure she'd put clean towels in the guest apartment.

"Fuller, you going to help?" Ed stood at the end of the walk, breathing hard, with his hand to his mouth to direct the sound.

"Yes, my apologies. I was speaking with the housekeeper." He shrugged his shoulders, and in a matter of minutes, Ed Murray, the driver and Fuller had the suitcases, crates, and boxes lined on the sidewalk, ready to haul into the house and up the stairs. Fuller paid the driver and watched a minute as he drove away, the tracks of his wheels shining in the wet cobblestones.

He lifted his most important possession, his overstuffed, locked, leather doctor's bag in one hand, and a valise in the other and turned toward the house. Following in his footsteps, with a heavy box in his arms, was Ed, his arms straining with the effort. They dumped their load on the floor near the stairway and went out for more. At last, the luggage was carried inside and taken upstairs to the two rooms that Edward had given him. There was a connecting door between them; one he would use for a bedroom, and the other for a sitting room.

Fuller looked around with interest; there was a fireplace with a marble mantle, a huge bed and two chairs in the bedroom. He turned the white ivory doorknob and walked through to the other room. Against the back wall, near the window stood a large desk and padded chair. The side wall was lined with shelves, and Fuller was very pleased. The windows were bare of curtains. He turned to his friend.

"Eddie, this is perfect. Where did you find this old house? How much is it going to cost me to keep the fires going? And, who's that sweet lady who answered the door?" He opened one

53

of the boxes and started taking out books. He turned with a small tome in his hand when he received no answer to his questions.

"Eddie?"

His friend at last grinned and spoke. "It took me a full week to find this place; one of the men at the hospital recommended it. It was partially furnished; you'll find except for my rooms across the hall, it's empty. The rug cost a fortune, and I expect full payment for it." Fuller looked down at the multi-colored carpet covering the center of the room, while about one foot near the walls was bare and showed a wooden surface.

Ed sighed. "I still owe the bank for the medical equipment. I bought only what was necessary. I figured the surgery and waiting room were more important than the house. The metal file cabinet was donated by one of the interns; he left San Francisco for Montana and couldn't take his furnishings with him. He gave us that bed you'll sleep on and the chairs. He hated the fog and damp air that rolls in from the sea. As for Fanny Bolade, she lost her husband to a stomach wound and has no family. He was a worker at the shipping docks and fell onto a spike. I did what I could, but he passed during surgery. She couldn't pay my fee, so I told her she could work the debt by cooking and cleaning, and she just sort of stayed. It's hard for her to go up and down the stairs, so I try to take care of my own rooms." He gave Fuller a speculative look and coughed. "The water closet is down the hall, and we'll have to set a schedule for its use. I like to bathe at night, after a hard day's work. You can use the one downstairs if you prefer it. I have it furnished for the patients; it's larger and fully equipped."

"Thanks, I'll see about it when I've settled in a few days. I'll make arrangements at the bank to help pay your debt; after all, it's half mine, isn't it? I'll make out a budget for the monthly food and expenses to pay for my own entertainment and clothing and other things I need. Have you hired a nurse or receptionist to help with the patients and keep the records of visits and medicines?"

"Yes, a young woman who's been thoroughly trained in medicine, but she's not too clever with the paper work. I've had to correct several mistakes. We'll have to keep a sharp eye on the records; go over the monthly accounts for each patient. Her name's Hyacinth Lorraine, likes to be called Cindy, has a French background, I think. She's pretty tight-lipped about her past. Comes from New Orleans, has a boyfriend named Zeke Burton. Zeke works on the docks, tall, burly fellow with arms like logs, dark skin. She lives with her sister, Marilynne, a waitress at the Chinese restaurant near the wharf. A pretty brunette, with dark eyes. I've taken her out a few times to the theater and dinner. Well, I guess I should let you settle in; Fanny will have dinner ready in an hour or so. After I eat, I spend about an hour or so with my patients at St. Michael's Hospital on Cedar Hill Lane. It's not far, easily walking distance in good weather." He started to leave, but Fuller stopped him.

Fuller set the book he'd been holding on the table and took out his wallet. He took a few paper bills from his wallet and a piece of paper. "This should take care of the first month's household expenses, until we can settle into a routine. The paper has the name and address of my parents in Colorado and my brother at the barracks at Fort Riley in Kansas. So, you'll have a record in case something happens to me."

Ed laughed. "What do you expect to happen in the city? We're as safe as in any big town." But, he took the money and paper and stuffed them in his pocket. "I'm glad you decided to take up my offer to practice in San Francisco; I thought you'd go to Denver to be near your folks."

"I'll tell you when we have more time. Thanks. I'll soon find my way around. After all, I spent a year in Europe, didn't I?" He chuckled. "Growing up as I did in the wilderness, you tend to take precautions against dangerous critters." He shrugged. "Go on, Eddie, I know you're impatient to get to your own affairs. I'll drill Fanny and make my way to the exam room for afternoon rounds. I want to visit the hospital and present my credentials to the authorities. Wish me luck. It's my first attempt to practice on my own."

Ed bounded down the stairs and out the door; his usual exuberance familiar to Fuller, who picked up the book he had set aside and started to fill his shelves.

Six

Fuller emptied the last box of books, glad to be finished lifting the heavy medical tomes, his favorite mysteries and numerous volumes of poetry. He hoped that Ed didn't tease him again about his love for poetry. He'd learned to appreciate the medium as a boy when he read *King Arthur and the Knights of the Round Table*, one of his father's books. He also had several of William Shakespeare's plays. He used his shirt sleeve to dust them off before putting them on the shelves. There was space left for more, and he sighed. If he was to help Ed with the debt, it would take him a long time to fill all the shelves.

He continued emptying his bags and boxes of the items inside. He was pleased to see that the two small water-color paintings crafted by his mother were intact. He made a note to ask Fanny for some hooks and a hammer. He held the first one above the fireplace; it showed the mountains near twilight with the snowy crevasses reflecting the pink glow from the setting sun. He put it down and took the other to the wall above his desk and imagined it there. It depicted a meadow covered with verdant grass and wild flowers: pink, yellow, and scarlet, with a predominance of white blossoms in the foreground. In the background stood a line of cottonwoods and willows, with a tumbled-down cabin half-hidden by the trees. As he worked, he began to smell delicious aromas from downstairs sifting up through the old house and knew that Fanny was preparing dinner. He was feeling hungry. Finally, his clothes were put away in drawers or hanging in the closet nook, and all the boxes and bags were empty. He shoved the bags on a top shelf. The boxes he took downstairs either to be thrown in the furnace to be burned or used again and almost bumped into a woman coming from the surgery.

He stood, the boxes in his hand, and his eyes gazed up and down her person. She was dressed in a neat, white shirt buttoned modestly to the collar with a small pin at the neck; the full black skirt hung from a shiny belt around her waist to just above her ankles. She had scuffed black shoes. His eyes went back up the almost boyish figure to the plain face and brown hair pulled severely to the back of her neck.

"Well, have you seen enough, sir?" she asked, a glow of anger in her eyes.

"Excuse me, I was surprised to see someone. Are you here to see the doctor? I believe he's gone to the hospital to see a patient." He shifted the boxes in his arms and finally put them on the floor. "I'm Doctor Fuller Hadley; perhaps I could help with your problem."

It was her turn to rake her eyes from the top of his dark brown hair and gray eyes to the brown shoes on his feet.

"Dr. Hadley? But, you're not at all what I expected. I was sure you were older and quite bald, with missing teeth," she said rather sarcastically.

Fuller was shocked and saw the gleam in her eyes. He could smell the faint scent of flowers drifting from her body or hair. He took in a deep breath and waited for her to continue.

"Hello. I'm Cindy, or more correctly, Hyacinth Lorraine, Dr. Murray's nurse and office clerk. Did you have a nice trip from Colorado?"

"Cindy? I'm pleased to meet you." He quickly reassessed his thoughts of the woman as he held out his hand. She hesitated a moment and shook his hand. Hers was soft and slightly damp. He withdrew a few steps; he would be working with her every day. That meant she was out of bounds as far as their relationship was concerned. "Yes, I had a charming visit with my parents and grandmother." He sighed. "I'll miss the sight of the distant mountains and the fresh, clean air, but I'm satisfied with what I've seen of San Francisco so far. Do you know where I can put these boxes?"

She glanced at the boxes and laughed. "Down in the basement would be a good place. Take that door near the kitchen range; it leads down into the bowels of the house. Fanny can tell you where." She brushed past him and returned to the room from which she had come. He took a step forward and saw that it must be the waiting room, for there were several chairs lining the far wall and a filing cabinet in the corner, with a green potted plant sitting on top. A large desk and chair stood in the corner. He picked up the boxes and headed toward the room from which the delicious smells emanated.

Fanny Bolade was standing at the stove humming a gay tune under her breath and stirring a pot on the burner, her body swaying to the music she heard in her head.

Fuller spoke softly, hoping not to startle the woman. "Mrs. Bolade, that smells awfully good. And, I'm ready for some food." He watched closely as the woman turned, the oversized spoon in her hand. She moved so quickly that a drop of red liquid fell onto the floor.

"Oh, drat." She went to the table, put the spoon down and took a cloth to wipe the spill from the floor. She turned impatiently. "Did you want something, Dr. Hadley?" Her quick eyes saw the boxes, and she frowned.

"Why, yes. I'd like to get rid of these boxes. Miss Lorraine says there's a basement that has space for them. Is that the door?" He nodded his head toward a door to the side of the stove.

Her eyes followed his, and she stepped to the door, opened it and leaned in. A switch clicked, and the darkened rectangle lighted, revealing a stairwell leading into the depths of the house. "Just put the boxes in the corner near the furnace, if you please. I'll have Silas take care of it when he comes. He's gone to the wharf to see if one of the fishing boats has come in with fresh salmon. I do love the taste of salmon." She looked strangely at Fuller. "Do you like fish? Some people are allergic to shellfish. You tell me if you can't eat certain things. I'd hate for Dr. Ed to have to use his pills and liquids on his partner." She burst out laughing; and Fuller couldn't help it. He laughed with her. "You'd best watch your steps on the stairs. You'll see the switch to turn off the light when you come back up." She nodded in a matter-of-fact manner and went back to stirring the pot on the stove.

Hearing Fanny humming happily, Fuller made his way cautiously down the stairs while holding the boxes securely in his arms and came out into a large room filled with wash tubs and a few shelves holding jars of fruits and vegetables. He could see a cord strung across the room, from which hung some sheets and other items. Apparently the basement was used on inclement days for laundry of bed linens and clothes used in the surgery. He set the boxes in a corner near the furnace and looked more closely at the room. There were two small windows near the ceiling letting in a dim light. He looked out and could see they were level with the sidewalk and grassy yard.

Returning to the brighter and more welcoming kitchen, he turned off the single bulb illuminating the lower portion of the house, closed the door securely after him and looked around. It wasn't a large room and seemed sparsely furnished. The shelves on one wall held only a few dishes; the kitchen utensils hung from pegs; he could see several empty pegs, indicating a need for more. Only a small table stood against the opposite wall for the use of the cook. A couple of straight-back, cane-bottom chairs stood beside it.

"Do you have everything you need, Mrs. Bolade? I've just arrived, as you know, and haven't had time to help with the furnishings. Ed has had to do it all alone, I'm afraid."

Fanny gazed around and nodded her head. "I could sure use another skillet, a Dutch oven and a few small pans. And, a rolling pin might be nice. Dr. Ed said it might take a while

61

before he could afford to buy more. He said the surgery and office supplies were more important. Don't you worry, Dr. Hadley, I've enough for now. Have to make do with what a person has sometimes. I go grocery shopping once a week and to the fish market on a Monday." She stirred her pot of soup and turned back to him. "You didn't say whether you were allergic to shellfish."

"No, I'm not allergic to anything as far as I know. I have some preferences for certain foods, but I'll try not to trouble you with my odd habits. I do like to eat out occasionally; I'll tell you when I won't eat in if I have a chance. I suppose Ed eats at the hospital when he's working there?"

"Yep, that he does. Many times I have to put the food in the oven to keep warm, or throw it away. A waste of food, says I, but I guess doctors don't have no regular hours like most folks. Now, you scoot along, sir; I got work to do." She waved her hand at him.

"Thank you, Mrs. Bolade," he said, as he turned down the hallway toward the waiting room. Miss Lorraine was hunched over the desk, the tip of her tongue in the side of her mouth, as though she were trying to solve a problem. She looked up and frowned when he stepped into the room. He cleared his throat.

"Hello, Miss Lorraine, is there something I can help you with?" he asked politely as he strode toward the desk. The sun was shining brightly through the window, and he thought one of the first things needed were curtains or shades to dim the light.

"Oh. Dr. Hadley. I can't seem to make these figures match. I know Mrs. Parmenter paid her bill last week but don't see it marked in this column." She held a pencil in one hand and was running a finger down the figures in the ledger.

"Let me look." He stepped close to the desk, and she flipped the ledger around so he could look at the numbers and words on the page. He drew up a chair and sat. The fragrance he'd smelled before tickled his nostrils, and he tried to ignore it. "What's the number you're looking for?" He glanced up and caught a speculative expression in her eyes. She quickly withdrew and handed him the pencil.

"A dollar and fifteen cents. Mrs. Parmenter had a scratch on her arm; she said from her cat; but Ed said it was more like her husband did it; she's been in several times with bruises and cuts. The women who live in the tenements have a hard life, and some of the husbands drink. Ed says there's nothing we can do if it's a minor thing. He calls in the police if a life is threatened or the injury is serious. You'll get used to it in time."

While she was talking, Fuller was running his eyes down the columns of figures but didn't see the name Parmenter or a figure of one dollar and fifteen cents.

"I don't see it here. Go ahead and put it down and add the figures again to see if they are correct. Do the people usually pay the whole amount, or does Ed accept other things in barter?"

"Oh, yes, we get a lot of chickens, and butter or vegetables. It troubles me because then I worry that the children and women aren't eating enough. But, they're a proud lot; Ed never refuses the items; says at least we get something. Some of the people never pay." She sighed again, wrote the amount of Mrs. Parmenter's payment and totaled the column, while Fuller watched.

Her eyes glowed when she finished, and he knew her columns matched. She looked up at him, apparently satisfied.

"How do you know the value of a chicken or the vegetables?"

"Fanny's useful in that regard; she does the shopping and knows the price of things. Silas knows the price of hardware and clothing. Sometimes we might get a jar of buttons or a discarded pair of shoes." She laughed. "You'll learn soon enough."

"I'm sure I will. If you're finished with your paperwork, perhaps you'll show me around the surgery? The people will be coming soon, and I don't want to appear completely ignorant on my first day." He smiled charmingly, and the nurse rose to oblige him.

He spent the next half hour getting familiar with the instruments, the files and the medicines in the large glass cabinet. She showed him the linen closet and the receptacle for used bandages. Fanny called them in to eat, and as he was spooning a morsel of soup into his mouth, Ed came in the door, his hair tousled and his coat speckled with dark spots. Fuller rose to greet him and the men talked of the patients that were expected that afternoon.

As the door was closed on the last patient, Fuller sighed with relief. He and Ed discussed the charts of the patients and wrote down the diagnoses and medicines prescribed. Cindy cleaned the rooms and went home. Fanny called them to supper, a roast beef, with mustard greens, potatoes and spiced beets, and a berry cobbler for dessert. Over the coffee, they continued their discussion of the afternoon, and at last Fuller went to his rooms, exhausted but pleased with his first day. He straightened his room and set out the clothes he would wear on the morrow. He had learned long ago to be prepared for emergencies in the middle of the night. He put his medical bag near the door in case it was needed and went to bed.

Seven

The next morning after an early breakfast, Ed accompanied Fuller to the hospital, where he made an appointment to meet with the head surgeon and officials and obtain the necessary privileges for any future patients to be admitted to the hospital. An orderly was assigned to him, and he was taken into the rooms in which he would work and shown the dining accommodations and other facilities. He observed the work of a surgeon from the balcony over the operating theater. He ate dinner in the dining facility near the hospital kitchen and met several interns and nurses, introduced himself and selected his food from the line of meats and vegetables. As he glanced around the room, it all became as familiar to him as his home in the pine forest of Colorado. The friendly interns told him stories of favorite restaurants and hotels, and where he might find entertainment or pleasure in his leisure hours.

Soon, his mind was a jumble of names: the Hibernia Bank, where he could withdraw or deposit money; the best clothing stores; the Palace Hotel; the Bella Union, where a pleasant night might be spent away from the scent and sight of patients; the Public Library; and the street cars pulled by cables and steam engines.

One intern, whose name Fuller learned was Tom Trifold, a charming young man who was a native of California, told him to be careful if he visited the Barbary Coast for entertainment, and his companion cautioned him about the pretty waiter girls who dispensed liquor and other services. Tom volunteered to accompany him on his first visit, and Fuller agreed to meet him on their next mutual day off work.

He went to the reception area for the hospital staff and waited until his name was called for his appointment. The room seemed to be filled with full-bearded or mustachioed men with sober faces and neat suits. Fuller admired one gentleman's silver-colored vest. He took out his credentials when asked and answered their questions about his classes, his training and his former teachers. He was surprised to find that they knew about his birthplace and home at Sweetwater Springs.

One ancient man, whose wrinkled face and snow-white hair reminded him of his late grandfather, gazed at him through watery eyes and rose from his seat. The other men watched as the gentleman peered at Fuller over his spectacles.

"You the son of Joe Hadley?"

"Yes, I am, sir." Fuller blinked at the question. He hadn't told them his father's name, only where he lived.

"I spent a few nights at your father's station once," he said. "It was in '71 or '72, before the stages stopped running, and the railroad tracks covered the land. There was an Indian there, liked to smoke a pipe; had a blanket around his shoulders, and spoke in a deep voice. You were just a child, barely old enough to ride a horse. I remember the spring and the creek, and the far distant mountain range. Had a terrible storm during the night. What ever happened to that old Injun? Is he still around, must be a hundred if he's alive." He chuckled, "I'm not so far from that age myself."

"No, sir, Standing Tree died when I was about twelve years old during a mustang hunt, tracking for my father. Did you know Roland Abernathy, the animal handler? His son married my sister, Jannette. They live in the old station house. My parents and grandmother live in a fine white house a ways from the barn."

"Well. Well. No, I didn't catch the names of the employees, just your parents. So. They're still there. And, the mountains, of course. Prettiest sight I ever saw, those mountains seen from your father's stage station." He turned toward the other men sitting behind the table who had control of Fuller's future. "Don't need to talk no longer, men. A son of Joe Hadley is alright in my estimation." He turned back to Fuller. "What was it that old Injun called your ma?"

"He called her Scarred Woman because of the burn scar on her face." Fuller took a quick glance at the other men and saw the interest in their eyes at that information.

"Yes. Yes. Scarred Woman. I remember now. She's still around, you say? She was a wonderful cook. Made the best apple pie I ever ate." He sat down and bowed his head as though lost in his thoughts of the past.

Fidel MacDermit, the head of the surgery department,

paused a moment as though gathering his thoughts and stood to shake hands. "We'll be in touch, Dr. Hadley. Thank you for your time."

Fuller rose, shook hands with all the men and left the room, carrying his credentials in a small satchel in one hand. He left the building by the front entrance and walked back to his new home. He couldn't tell from their expressions or their gestures whether he was accepted or not. He thought it strange that one of the men in control of his future had ridden on a stage through his father's property so long ago.

Three days later, his new friend Tom Trifold, his partner Ed Murray and he spent a pleasant night on the Barbary Coast, drinking and taking in the delights of the local entertainment provided for single young men. Tom had found women of the night for each of them, and Fuller left the others at some point and ended in a room above the dance hall. The woman, Beryl, wore a thin dress in which her nipples could be seen as she flaunted her large breasts; the hem was above the knee, and she wore black stockings and white bow-tied garters with black shoes with pointed toes. Fuller delighted in chasing her around the room until he captured her and stripped the garters from her limbs and put one in his coat pocket before she succumbed to his mocking laughter.

The next day, his head aching and his eyes blood-shot, he opened the mail and read a formal acceptance of his request for hospital privileges. He assisted Ed during office hours and wrote a long letter to his parents telling them of the endorsement and a few details of the practice and his new home. He mentioned the old man and his visit to Sweetwater Station in

1871, but didn't write of his trip to the Barbary Coast. He put the garter away in his handkerchief drawer to remember his initiation into the nightlife of the West Coast.

Eight

On his first full day after receiving his official papers from the hospital authorities, Fuller rose before six o'clock, ate a hearty breakfast and walked to the hospital. The weather was fair, and he took a deep breath of the damp air coming off the ocean. There was also the smell of humanity on the move, very different from his home in the mountains. He opened the side door to the hospital and went upstairs to the doctors' locker room. There were two men inside who seemed to be arguing, but he didn't stop. He put his medical bag on the bench beside the locker assigned to him and pulled out his key to open the lock. He noticed the men were silent.

"Heh, that's Bill's locker," one of the men said. Fuller turned to him.

"Bill? But, this is the number they gave me when I received my letter of acceptance." He looked at the number and drew a sheet of paper from his vest pocket. "Yes. Number A24. That's it." He took the key and inserted it into the lock, and the door swung open.

The man who had spoken crossed the room and saw that the locker was empty. He looked puzzled. "But, what's happened to Bill Walworth? Lee Roy, do you know?" The other man shook his head, but he didn't question Fuller's ownership of the locket. He stepped forward.

"My name's Terrill, Lee Roy Terrill. I'm a pediatrician, been here four years. Came from Bakersfield. Some might say that's not very far; but for a small town boy, it's a long ways. Don't you know anything about Bill Walworth? He was here on Friday, as always, an obstetrician. We make a good team; he delivers them, and I raise them." He grinned, his ears turning red. "Their parents and me, that is."

"I'm Fuller Hadley, surgeon. My folks live in Colorado, but I've been away for a long time. My friend Edward Murray and I have a place a few blocks away. We have our own practice, but I've obtained permission to bring my patients here and use the operating theater when necessary. I don't know this Bill you're talking about." He put his hat and outer coat in the locker, along with a sack that Fanny had given him with some crackers and an apple. She'd told him he might need some food before he finished his work. Fuller didn't expect much work today, but he didn't want to upset her. Ed often took a bag of crackers, cheese and an apple in case he needed to stay late. Fuller had brought his father's old Army canteen with him from Colorado, and he placed it on the shelf.

The other man stepped forward. "I know Ed Murray; he told us he had a friend from medical school coming. Glad to know you. My name's Linley, Joab Linley. I'm a bone doctor, an orthopedist. Lee Roy, I'm headed to see what's happened to Bill; I'm sure if he was leaving he'd have told us. Say, Hadley, you like to play poker? Some of the fellows get together when we have time."

"I've played a game or two before." The man called Lee Roy gazed at him as though to assess his character. He had dark hair, dark eyes, and was clean shaven. Fuller noticed that Linley was taller and had a full beard. They both wore dark trousers and white shirts with no ties.

"You go ahead, Joab, find out what happened to Bill. I'll show Hadley around the place."

Fuller finished at the locker, locked it and put the keys in his pocket. He turned.

"What's that round thing you put in there? I've seen the Army's canteen, but I ain't never seen one like that. Looks old." Lee Roy led Fuller out and shut the door behind him. As he turned to go left down the hallway, a man rushed past them.

"Ezra, what's happened to Bill? His locker was empty, and this man has the key. Name's Hadley, from Colorado."

The man turned and walked backwards down the hall, as though he had no time to linger. "Bill Walworth? Why, he quit. He said he had a letter that his father's dying, and he's gone to Ohio. I can't stay; I'm expected in the laboratory. You know how impatient old Stallingworth gets."

Fuller watched as the man almost ran down the hall. They turned in the opposite direction, and Lee Roy started talking about the boy he was treating with burns on his body from a boiling pot of water fallen from the stove. The Confederate Army canteen was forgotten as they parted company at the door

73

to the surgery, where Ed was waiting for him.

*****

The days and weeks seemed to fly by as Fuller fell into the routine of breakfast, trips to the hospital to visit with patients, afternoon office hours, evening meals and weekends or nights spent in frivolous entertainment with his new friends, interspersed with trips to the tonsorial parlor and the library. Neither man had the funds to buy all the medical books and magazines to remain abreast of the recent advances in their field of endeavor. He set up an account at the Hibernia Bank on Jones Street and borrowed a small sum to help Ed pay off his debt for the house and surgery furnishings.

Giving in to the pull of concert saloons and gambling dens, he was soon able to pay off his personal loan, and his account began to grow.

On his second day in the big house, Fuller had learned of Silas Pitt, the handyman, who came once a week to do the heavy cleaning and brought cords of wood for the fireplaces and kitchen range. He was willing to run errands or accompany Fuller or Ed to the furniture warehouses, and slowly, a piece at a time, Fanny's kitchen utensils were expanded, more chairs and small tables appeared in the rooms, and a pretty flowered lamp was added to the doctor's waiting room.

Silas was interested in the construction of the buildings for the Midwinter's fair to be held the next year in Golden Gate Park. He told Fuller that he'd been to the park several times looking for work but hadn't been accepted. He admitted he had no skills for carpentry or machinery. One day, Fuller decided to visit the site and came home full of images of structures being built, cables strung for electricity, ditches and canals being dug, and foliage being planted. He and Silas put their heads together and drew diagrams to show Ed and Fanny how it would be. They read the newspaper and eagerly awaited the great event.

Fuller met Zeke Burton, Cindy's boyfriend, a hearty fellow, who seemed a perfect foil for the tall, slender woman. He was burly and clean-shaven, with side whiskers and a handle-bar mustache. The six of them, Edward and Cindy's sister Marilynne, Cindy and Zeke, and Fuller and a waitress friend of Marilynne's named Dahlia visited Chinatown, and Fuller got his first sample of the opium dens, but decided he must leave it alone or his medical skill would suffer. His association with Dahlia lasted a short two weeks, for he had no desire to settle down with one woman.

He came home one evening in July after an exhausting day at the hospital to find Cindy and Ed quarreling at the desk in the office. Ed was red-faced and his hair stood up as though he had run his hand through it several times in frustration. Cindy was crying and subdued. It took a while to ascertain the problem. It seemed that Cindy had forgotten to mail a check to the building and loan association from which Ed had purchased the house, and they were two months behind in the mortgage payments. It was too late in the day to visit the bank, and the next day was a Friday.

"Damn, Cindy, can't you get anything right? I trusted you with the bankbook, and now I'll get a reputation as a free-loader, or worse, they'll think I'm overextended in my financial affairs. I can't afford to lose my good name and position at the hospital. If it gets around that I'm not paying the bills on time, MacDermit will give me a lecture on irresponsibility. Fuller, can you help me with a loan until we find what she did with the check she wrote? It didn't make its way to the bank." He thrust his hand through his hair.

"I'll give you what you need, but it'll make me short this month. I'll have to buckle down and not leave the house for a while. I'll have Fanny make a sandwich and something for my dinner each day instead of eating in the dining facility. Where did you last see the check? Did you put it in the envelope? Come on, girl, try to remember." Fuller began to rummage through a stack of papers on the desk, hoping it was hidden from sight, but not lost.

"I've already looked, Fuller. She says she mailed it, but the bank didn't receive it. I asked. And, I have to go back to the hospital. Old Mr. Fitzhugh is dying, and I promised his wife and children I'd be there with them tonight." He glared at Cindy, and her tears flowed harder.

"You go to the hospital, Ed. I'll see what I can do here. Cindy, is Zeke coming to walk you home? When is he supposed to be here?" Fuller was still searching through the papers. Ed dashed from the room, picked up his hat from the hall rack and they heard him greet Zeke as he came in the front door. The door closed behind him.

"Cindy, get your hat and gloves and go home. I'll see you tomorrow. Hello, Zeke, she's ready to leave. It's a nice night for walking. I just came from the hospital. A little warm, but a cool breeze is blowing from the south." He looked up to see a puzzled look on Zeke's face. He obviously had observed the tear-streaked face of his lover. But, there was nothing Fuller could do. He turned back to the desk and heard the front door close with a soft click. He began to organize the papers, letters, bank drafts from the patients and invoices from vendors and tradesmen.

He made several stacks, separating each item according to its importance. He was hungry and tired. The house was silent, and he occasionally heard a tree limb rub against the wall of the house as the wind continued to blow from the south. The creaks and groans of the old house didn't bother him as he worked. Finally, he worked his way through the chaos, and halfway stuck in a crack at the side of the desk was the closed and stamped envelope addressed in Cindy's neat handwriting to the Claremore Building and Loan Association. He didn't open it, but knew it must be the check in question.

He pulled out the ledger that contained the household accounts and went through the columns of figures. He found two mistakes and groaned. It was obvious that Cindy was a fine nurse and compassionate with the patients, but hopeless as a bookkeeper. He found five patient envelopes with payments not recorded. He opened the sealed envelopes and recorded the contents in the ledger or answered the queries. This gave them added funds for the household accounts for the next week and Fanny's salary. They were solvent again for a while. He filed them all neatly and, leaving the desk tidy and clean, went to the kitchen to eat a solitary, cold supper. He took the stairs slowly, his feet dragging from exhaustion and tumbled into bed without setting out his clothing for the next day or brushing his teeth.

He was halfway asleep when he remembered but didn't get back up. He was too tired. The next day, he visited the loan association as soon as it opened, explained the discrepancy and deposited the funds for the current month.

He talked to Ed, and they both agreed that Cindy would have to be replaced as a bookkeeper. They put their heads together, and Fuller agreed to take over the paperwork until they could afford to hire a secretary or accountant. Since his funds weren't needed to pay the mortgage, he went for an early dinner at a Chinese restaurant he frequented and spent the rest of the day going through the files, while Ed visited their patients at the hospital. The patient charts were his next challenge, and he spent the weekend sorting them out.

When Cindy was told her services were no longer needed in the office, but desperately needed in the surgery, she blinked and began to cry again. It took both Ed and Fuller to assure her that they held no ill will towards her, and peace was restored.

Fuller discovered later that Ed had broken his relationship with Marilynne after she quarreled with her sister, and within a month, he had found another girlfriend by the name of Melody Grant. The relationship didn't last long, and no girl was chosen to replace her. Ed worked hard and long hours, seemingly content, and Fuller ceased to think about it.

Cindy seemed withdrawn, and one morning in September came in late, her eyes red-rimmed and bloodshot, and told them of a quarrel she'd with Zeke the night before. It seemed that she had returned from work and found him in bed with Marilynne. Fuller wasn't as shocked as was Ed; he'd sensed some conflict between the sisters for some time. When they finished for the day and Cindy had gone home and Ed to the hospital to visit the old man who was dying, Fuller decided to take an inventory of the medicine cabinet.

He counted the bandages, cleaned and sterilized the instruments and placed them in their cabinet drawers or trays. He carefully recorded each bottle and box and found a bottle of laudanum missing. Thinking it had been misplaced, he went through every shelf, drawer, box and bottle, but it was not to be found. He waited up for Ed, and when he arrived told him of the discrepancy. Ed shook his head.

"I haven't used it since I stitched little Jimmie Tatum's arm. You remember, Fuller, the boy who fell on the sidewalk and was brought in by his father. I put the bottle back on the shelf after his father carried him home. I know I did."

"I didn't use it today; there was Mrs. Tamika, but she refused anything; said she could handle the pain without drugs. She was emphatic, and I had no other cases after her." Fuller gazed around the room. "I've looked everywhere it would be, Ed. Wait." He shook his head and frowned. "Now that I think about it, I saw Cindy standing near the cabinet just before she left." With a scowl on his face, he grabbed his coat and bag and left, calling, "You get some sleep, Ed, I may need you later," and rushed from the house.

Cindy and Marilynne's apartment was within walking distance, and he ate up the blocks with a long stride, his heart pounding and his fears mounting as he climbed the steps to the front door. It seemed every light in the house was burning, and there was a horse-drawn carriage at the curb. The door was opened by a frantic, hand-wringing Zeke.

"Come in, Fuller; she's dead," he said in a deep, mournful voice. "Marilynne found her when I brought her home from the restaurant. She was lying on the floor of the kitchen. I called to the policeman on the corner, and he's with her now. I don't know what to do; she seemed so calm when I left her after the argument last night. She told Mary she'd be alright. She was crying when I left; Mary was, too." He sat on a chair and stared at the wall.

Fuller raced into the kitchen and saw a policeman in uniform at the window. He started toward the woman on the floor.

"Hey, now. You can't come in here, sir." The civil official put out a hand and restrained Fuller as he moved toward Cindy.

"I'm a doctor." He pulled out his wallet showing his card. The policeman read it and handed it back.

"It's alright, then, Doc. I've sent for the coroner and the ambulance, but I guess it won't hurt nothing for you to look at her. There's no bullet or knife wounds; looks like she took her own life. I sent the sister upstairs; she's hysterical. The boyfriend's in the parlor; I guess you saw him. A lover's quarrel, looks like." He stopped as they heard the sound of a horn and people talking outside. "I'll go see if that's the ambulance." And the policeman left Fuller alone in the room.

Fuller felt of Cindy's pulse and took out his stethoscope. There was no heartbeat. She was lying flat in the same dress she had worn to work, and her face was serene. He looked around and saw no bottle containing the drug. He assumed the policeman had it. Suddenly, the room was full of people, the ambulance attendants, the coroner, Zeke, and a pale, haggard

Marilynne, sniffling into her handkerchief.

Zeke took her in his arms, and Fuller could see the intimate gesture for what it was. Cindy was right; they must have been lovers for some time. He cursed under his breath. If the man wanted to change allegiance from one sister to another, why hadn't he been honest about it?

Cindy was lifted onto the stretcher and carried from the house. The officials asked questions for an hour. Fuller could only say why he had come to the house: the missing bottle of laudanum. The policeman, whose name Fuller learned was Colin O'Dowell, took Fuller into an upstairs room, and the questions continued: How long had she worked for him? When was the last time he saw her? When did he discover the bottle missing? The coroner announced there would be a hearing and he should be there. Fuller agreed and at last was released and walked home.

It was much too late to awaken Ed or Fanny, so he undressed and crawled into his own bed, but his mind continued to summon images until exhaustion claimed him and he slept.

He rose the next morning and explained to Ed and Fanny as they ate breakfast. He told them they would all have to go to the coroner's inquest into the matter. They went on about their work, but the house seemed to mourn with them. The floors squeaked as usual, and the windows were streaked with the rain that fell on the next day. The sidewalk and the steps were covered with shallow puddles, and Fuller stepped around them as he walked home that evening.

Two days later, they attended the funeral, and Fuller spoke a few words with the woman's mother and brother. He dutifully attended the inquest and answered all the questions as truthfully as he could. Ed and Fanny also sat as though stunned and answered in quiet murmurs. The verdict was read, "Death by suicide." The newspaper carried a small article on the third page, and the matter passed from the public's conscious thoughts.

A couple of weeks later, Zeke and Marilynne were quietly married at the office of a Justice of the Peace and left San Francisco for Los Angeles where the mother and brother lived. Fuller attended the wedding, but neither Ed nor Fanny went. Marilynne, a tall, spare woman with a bow mouth and pencil thin eyebrows, wore a lacy open-sleeved gray dress, whose beaded bodice hung loosely at the waist and tapered into a trailing skirt. Her outfit was complemented by a large-brimmed black hat with a wide, white fluffy ribbon and feather at the brim that covered her dark hair. Her mother wore a black mourning dress, the only accessory a cameo pin at the neck.

Fuller talked to a local personnel agency, and they recommended several women whom he interviewed one by one in his office. Ed approved of his choice, and she arrived the next morning.

Miss Galena Fairchild, who was hired as a replacement, was as different from Hyacinth Lorraine as a person could be. Of average height and overweight, she was older and extremely efficient and mild-mannered. She had more than twenty years' experience working with an elderly gentleman who had been in practice in Yerba Buena before it was absorbed by San Francisco when it grew to its present size. Galena had never married and had no responsibilities outside of a black and white cat, which she cherished as though he was her child. She loved plants and flowers, and before the men realized what had happened, plants were strewn over every table and hanging from baskets in the corners of the waiting room. She happily watered and cared for them, and when a patient complained that plants weren't healthy, she went into a lecture on the healing effects of the greenery.

Fuller was no longer required to handle the paperwork, and Ed stopped worrying whether the tradesmen and mortgage would be paid on time. There was one small problem, however. Galena and Fanny frequently clashed over the care and feeding of the doctors. The problem came to a head on a wet, cold November morning, when Ed developed a cough and Fuller ordered him to take his own medicine and stay in bed. It was soon resolved when Fuller told the women to keep to their separate chores and responsibilities: Fanny in the kitchen and bedrooms; Galena in the surgery and office. Thus, the women ignored a certain strip between the rooms, and Fuller quietly cleaned and polished it when needed.

The winter was mild, and the fog off the ocean almost constant. The damp air brought many patients to the large white house as men, women and children coughed, sneezed, wheezed and complained of sore throats. The doctors spent much time in the tenements caring for those who couldn't come to the house. They spent almost every waking hour tending to the patients and were grateful when the epidemic was over and the sun again shone over the city by the bay.

Fuller received a letter from his father saying he was coming in May to see this fabulous fair that Fuller raved about.

On May the tenth, he arrived on the ferry from Oakland, Fuller met him and they rode a cab to the house, where Ed and Fanny were formally introduced. She cooked a special meal that evening of baked haddock with a tart sauce for dressing, and potatoes, cabbage with pieces of ham hock, spiced beets, green peas, and for desert, a cherry cobbler. Joe had never eaten such a splendid meal, he told her, and Fuller was pleased.

The next morning they arose early and prepared to cross to the park and take in the sights. They first visited the Palace of Fine Arts Building, and next the Agriculture and Horticulture Building created in the old California Missions style. Fuller explained to his father that he had read that most of the buildings were temporary and made of wood frames and wire mesh, covered with plaster and horsehair. Joe responded with skepticism and anxiety.

But, once he got inside, he forgot the exterior of the building, admired the three domes that let in light from the sun and examined the fruit stands heaped high with oranges, dates, figs, strawberries and artichokes from the hills and valleys of California.

"Would you look at this, son?" Joe asked, holding an artichoke in his hand. "Do you think Fanny could cook this for our meal? I've never seen anything like it. Do they sell them at the market?" He put it back on the stack and turned to the grapes, plump, juicy, purple and green ones, in clusters piled high and displayed with some kind of greenery he couldn't identify. "I wish Hannah could see all this produce. She'd love to eat some sweet grapes from the vine. I wonder if they'd grow in Colorado."

"I don't know, Papa, the altitude is probably too high."

Joe sighed and moved to the next stall and admired the other vegetables and fruit. "All this food makes me hungry. Do they have eating places in the park?"

Fuller laughed. "Come, Papa, we'll try the Japanese Tea Gardens. I've heard they have food."

They caught one of the man-pulled carts offered to the guests of the exposition, rode past the other buildings and came to what looked to Joe like an odd-shaped building poised on a hill. The man pulling the cart was dressed in the Japanese style, and Fuller tipped him generously. Joe's head swiveled from left to right as he took in the sights while walking to the tea house. They navigated paths lined with foliage, skirted ponds with golden fish, and amazed, they crossed over the moon bridge, where he could see the reflection of himself and the bridge in the water. A cool breeze swept through the foliage and disturbed Fuller's hair. He impatiently brushed it down with his hand. They sat and drank tea and ate tiny fish cakes, followed by a fortune cookie, and watched the pedestrians with interest. Fuller showed Joe how to open the treat, and inside was a small piece of paper. It said, "You will live with prosperity and gladness." Joe laughed so loudly that two women passing their table stared at him. He ducked his head and brought his hat down over his ears.

"Papa, it's only a piece of paper."

"I know, son, but how did the cookie bakers know what my future will be?" He glanced around him. "Are we supposed to eat them?"

"You can if you like. They make them by the hundreds, and

they have these little teasing messages in all of them." He opened his cookie and read, "The moon will guide you to fortune."

"See, Papa, it doesn't mean anything. Are you finished? I'd like to visit the emergency hospital. Ed said they have an ambulance. We sure need one in San Francisco; transportation for the patients is one of the biggest problems." They rose and paid for their meal, and Joe paused occasionally at a plant or flowering vine to admire the beauty and smell.

Fuller patiently waited at every stop, and at last they arrived at Lengfeld's Pharmacy, where he poked, examined and admired the clean and tidy appearance of the medical facilities. Joe gazed about him in awe and dutifully admired the ambulance, which appeared to him to be a tent on wheels. He waited at the side while Fuller climbed in and asked the attendant questions about the vehicle.

Each now satisfied with something that interested them, they passed the photographer's booth, and Joe bought a souvenir book of the fair. They had to wait while a parade passed them, the horns blasting, the drums drumming and the men marching, wearing bright red uniforms with gold appointments. The sun had set in the western sky, and it was getting dark and the air chilled. From a hill, they looked back at the buildings and towers and the high wheel of the amusement ride as the lights came on. Even Fuller was impressed.

"It's magical," Joe said. "I'm tired and hungry, but I'm glad I came." The electrical lights twinkled, and the sky lit up like a huge bonfire in the distance. "But, it doesn't compare with the stars and the moon," Fuller heard his father say, as they walked the rest of the way to his home.

The men sat in the waiting room of the surgery long into the night comparing sights and sounds, and finally, they climbed the stairs to their beds, where far in the distance, Fuller could hear the sound of fog horns, faint music and pedestrians as they passed on the sidewalk below. He had barely closed his eyes when a knock was sounded on the door. From long habit, he pulled on his robe and went to the door. It was an orderly from the hospital.

Quickly he ran upstairs, dressed and grabbed his bag and coat, for a heavy fog had rolled in from the sea. He returned later that morning just in time to wish his father God's speed as he prepared to catch the ferry to Oakland and the train for Colorado. He didn't follow him to the docks; he needed sleep.

"Farewell, my boy. Don't worry about me." Joe gave him a hug and turned to the cab that would take him to the ferry. Fuller watched him climb into the vehicle. The driver lightly touched the rump of the horse with the tip of his whip, and it moved down the hill and out of sight. With a heavy sigh, Fuller ate a quick meal that Fanny prepared and slept the afternoon away.

*****

During the fall and winter, Fuller received three letters from his father. Winnie Stafford had lost her second child, a stillborn boy, and Tater was devastated, but she was soon on the mend and healthy again. Janey was expecting her third and hoped it would be a girl. Ruth was suffering greatly from the pain in her knuckles and joints but didn't complain. Joe was able to sell five of the draft horses to the Army, and they requested mules if he could provide them. The saw mill was shut down during the inclement weather but would open again in the spring. He sent a check on his Denver bank, "for expenses," he wrote. Fuller was ashamed to admit the funds would be enormously useful, as they had treated no large amount of paying patients during the recent months. He made a payment on the mortgage, and Ed wrote to Joe and gently chastised him for sending the funds, although they were greatly appreciated.

Winter was followed by spring and summer, and it was winter again, and spring once more. Fuller couldn't believe the time had flown so swiftly. He had been in San Francisco four years. His life had fallen into a pattern that seemed endless. He discussed the matter with Ed, and they decided they needed a holiday. Ed took a month off, and then it was Fuller's turn. He caught the train in Oakland and was whisked to the beautiful mountains that he loved. Tater met him at the terminal in Denver in the surrey, and the fresh clean air, the scent of pine and spruce once more filled his lungs and heart with joy.

Nine

The Sweetwater Springs of 1897 wasn't changed much from the last time Fuller had visited his home. A few trees were missing, and others had grown to replace them. The house had been freshly painted, and a new house stood near the river and the saw mill. Almost the first thing he did when he arrived was saddle a chestnut mare and ride to his grandfather's favorite fishing hole, and there, the tension and stress of the last few months slowly melted away as he held the pole in his hand. He caught two brown trout and ate part of one for his supper, along with his mother's roast beef, potatoes with onions and corn on the cob.

Fuller sat at the table and looked at his family under the glow of the crystal chandelier in the dining room: Joe Hadley, stooped of shoulders, hair turned slightly gray, his face craggy and nut-brown from years in the wind and sun, except for his forehead that had been protected by his hat. His eyes were still sharp and clear. His mother, Hannah, had put on weight, and her face had grown wrinkled and sagged near the chin; the scar was puckered and red, as always. His grandmother had changed most of all; his observant eyes could tell she had lost weight and her eyes were almost blind, but her smile when she saw him was sweet, and the tears slid down her cheeks like a slow summer's rain. He determined to examine her if she would allow it.

The biggest surprise of all was his younger brother, Johnie, whom he hadn't seen since he was a youngster in faded denim trousers. He was tall and slender like their father, but his hair was fuzzy with blond curls and his eyes a dark brown. He held himself straight and stiff when they shook hands, and Fuller wondered if he resented the years of his absence when the other men had worked and tilled the soil, while he had enjoyed the more comfortable life of the city. But, after a few days, he realized that it was his normal manner, honed from his years in the Army.

Johnie lived with his wife, Vanessa, and two daughters, Petunia, called Pet, and Rosemary, called Rose, in the house near the river. It was a small clapboard house, only two bedrooms, and Fuller was amazed at the amount of blooming rose bushes in the garden. Pinks, yellows, and deep reds, the flowers were the special project of Vanessa, who was blonde with blue eyes. She laughingly told him that she had lived at so many barren Army posts that she needed the color to restore her soul every day. Johnie gave her an affectionate glance, and Hannah smiled.

That first night, Fuller felt awkward and a little remote as the family discussed events in their lives that he knew nothing about. He hesitated to burst forth with his own stressful life, for he knew they wouldn't understand, but the next day he and Joe went riding on a couple of saddle horses through the forest, and stopped under a huge Ponderosa pine. Joe dismounted and motioned for Fuller to step down.

"What's troubling you, son? Are you working too hard? Do you need money? I won't feel easy until I know that you're well and happy." It was the same Joe Hadley that Fuller had always known, charming, compassionate and thinking of others before himself.

He squatted on the ground, took a cigar from his pocket and lit it with a sulfur match. He took a deep breath of the smoke and blew it into the air, where it circled his head and drifted away.

"Papa, I've seen too much death; too much disease and heartache. I doubt you could understand, living peacefully here, what it's like, surrounded by humanity and strife. Gunshot wounds, knife wounds, cancers, open sores, fever and pain." He took another puff of his cigar and said, "So much pain, and I feel helpless to prevent it. When I first started, I had big dreams of curing the sickness and the sorrow, but I've found it's impossible. Sometimes, I fall into bed with my clothes on, too tired to make the attempt to undress. I feel so lonely and long for the sight of the mountains and the forest. It's a jungle in the city, full of wild animals called humans." He stopped talking and sat flat on the surface of the ground, gazing around him at the pine needles and the cones and round river rocks that had tumbled and washed down from the high places beyond the station and landed here in this place.

"But, you chose that life, son. I remember when you were small; you were restless, could never have stayed like Janey and Walter. You said you were stifled here. Does this mean that you want to come home and stay?" He gazed at Fuller with soulful eyes and a cautious look of hope.

Fuller laughed. "No, Papa, I don't want to stay. I could never be happy plowing the fields or working in the saw mill." He put his cigar on the ground and put out the flame with his shoe heel. He looked up sheepishly. "I needed to see the mountains again, instead of the street cars and the tall buildings and the foot traffic. Papa, do you remember when Standing Tree took me into the forest and showed me how to follow wolf tracks?"

Joe gave his son a strange look, his eyes somber and gleaming with remembrance. "Of course. I wasn't sure that you remembered; you were so young."

Fuller laughed, his eyes crinkling with fondness for his father. "Well, it's a little vague in my mind, but I remember what the old man said. He told me, 'Young boy take care of Yo Hadley and Scarred Woman when old; Yo Hadley my friend. Scarred Woman my friend. Big Father from across mighty river give Standing Tree smokes.' He pointed his finger at me and said, 'When Standing Tree gone from this place, you take care my friends.' I guess that was his only way to describe the affection and love he had for you. He left me with that trust, but I haven't kept my word. I've gone my own way and left the others to protect and support you. Am I too selfish, Papa, to want to help strangers, but not my own family?"

Joe Hadley rose to his fullest height and gazed around at the trees. It took him a moment to control his emotions. There was a strange look in his eyes that Fuller didn't understand.

"Selfish, maybe, a little wild, maybe, but I've always loved you for it. I was only eighteen when I went off to war. I saw the mangled bodies and deaths of my friends, boys I grew up with, men I met while training to be a soldier, the smoke of rifles and cannons, the sound of bullets hitting flesh and the crimson red of blood flowing like water from the bodies of the men." He turned and walked away.

Fuller watched him go and for the first time understood how it must have been; he'd laughed or ignored the tales of war and destruction of the eastern towns and villages when told of them. They had seemed so minor in his young life. Now, he heard the anguish in his father's voice as he spoke of those days. He looked at the ground and saw a tiny ground squirrel venture out from under a large stone and stand while it nibbled on a piece of brown nut. How simple life is for the animals of the forest, he thought. He heard a sound, and Joe was coming back. He straightened his shoulders.

"Son, I know you think I'm an old man, past my prime, but I've been where you are today. Maybe not in a hospital or a person's home, but I've seen the blood, the pain, the last dying breath of a man as he passes from this world into the next. When I came back from the war, my parents were despondent and sad. My older brother Luther had taken over the home farm and shut them out. My brother James was lost at Gettysburg. I've told you this before. I hoped for better for my children. I bought this property from the stage coach officials with the approval of the Territorial Governor when I realized that the stages would stop running. I wanted my parents to always have a home where they felt secure and safe. Someday, it'll belong to you, Janey, Walter and Johnie. When that time comes, you remember what I'm saying today. Even though you've chosen not to live here, it'll always be a part of you. It's my gift to you and your sister and brother; and to Walter, too, for he's lived here most of his life. He's earned his share in toil and sweat. Now, you enjoy your few short days in the sun and peace of the place and go back to where you're needed the most. Take care of those who are helpless and weak and blind to the sorrow of the world. Your mother and me, yes, and your grandmother, too, wouldn't want it any other way." He took out his white handkerchief and blew his nose. He put it back in his pocket.

"Now, enough of this sentimentality. Let's ride." He mounted his horse, and with a Rebel yell that would have shaken the snow off the mountain peaks if it had reached them, Joe trotted away, threading his way through the tree trunks and boulders with a skill and daring that Fuller admired. He pulled himself up on his own horse and trailed after him.

After a while they slowed the horses, Joe led him to the far boundaries of his property and Fuller was aware of the pride that his father felt in the land. It was his heritage, and he could appreciate the beauty of the nature as they rode. Joe pointed out landmarks, and at last they came to the box canyon. Fuller knew the legend of the black mustang stallion that had roamed this land when his father had first sighted him but had never been able to catch. He patted the neck of his mount, bred from a descendant of the eastern stallion given to his father by MacGregor and the mustang mare, Eva. It was the fourth or fifth generation of the line, but the horse had endurance and strength, and Fuller was at peace when he circled the spring and followed his father to the corrals.

Ten

The month that Fuller spent on his parent's farm seemed to fly by with wings. He spent his days riding, fishing and even taking a turn with a sick animal.

A man who introduced himself as Jake but didn't give his last name approached Fuller one afternoon several days into his visit. "Doctor Hadley, I got a question I want to ask of you."

"Go ahead, son." The boy was a beanpole, and barely old enough to wield a razor.

"This calf, well, it's got the bloats, and you being a doctor, I 'spect it's alright to ask you to help."

"And you're unfamiliar with bloat." Fuller took a deep breath. Bloat, not fun.

"Didn't say that. Done it lots of times, but the calf is worse this time, and you being a doctor, I best ask you and give you the chance to work your magic." Jake nodded, his eyes showing hope that Fuller would agree to this.

"Bloat. A calf with bloat." Fuller repeated the words.

"Yes, sir, about two months old."

"Well, Jake, let's get to looking at that calf. Maybe together we can work out that bloat and make that calf happy."

They were at the corral by then, and Jake clambered over the fence, one booted foot into the rails, then throwing the other over, and landing with a thump on the other side.

Fuller made his way through the gate. He groaned when he saw the calf, but together they got the job done, and hopefully, it would be the last animal he was asked to doctor on the farm.

As they left the corral Fuller asked, "How did you come to be working here, Jake?"

The youngster looked up with a grin, his eyes twinkling. "I grew up in an orphanage in Denver. I run away. Mr. Johnie saw me walking down the road. I tried to hide behind a tree, but he pulled me out. I thought he'd take me to the sheriff, but he gave me a job."

"My brother gave you a job working with the cattle?"

"Yes, sir. I been here 'bout six months now. He told me he joined the Army when he was about my age. I been thinking on it, but I don't guess I'd cotton to the army life, myself." He kicked at a pebble on the ground. "I gotta go, Dr. Hadley, 'preciate your help with the calf." With a wave he headed to the barn.

Fuller thoughtfully shook his head, impressed with his brother's unexpected compassion. Perhaps he'd misjudged the man. He'd certainly earned the loyalty of this boy.

He spent a day at the saw mill watching the men as they fed the timber onto the crank-driven saw and made boards of all sizes. The shed roof which covered the saw table was made of pine, with four poles to hold it up. The open air rang with the sound of grinding wood, the massive blade eating the spruce hauled by wagon to be fused into sheets of plywood.

The saw fell quiet for an hour at midday, and the men gathered at a rough, wooden table set under a towering tree to partake of a filling meal. The silence of the nearby woods was tangible after hours of the saw chewing through its daily diet of hardwood. Johnie finished quickly, moving to supervise a load of logs arriving at the mill. Joe introduced Fuller to the new hand before heading off to the house, saying he needed to speak with his wife.

"Rex Kane." The mill worker held out his hand as he pulled a cloth cap off his head, removed bulky goggles from his eyes and brushed a layer of sawdust from his face with his sleeve. "I heard we had a famous doctor on the premises."

Fuller laughed and shook hands. "Famous? Hardly. I'll own up to doctor, however. Fuller Hadley at your service."

"What do you think of the new steam engine?" It sat puffing away merrily off to the side. The firebox under the boiler was open to allow the water to cool. "I've been impressed with your father's setup. I feel fortunate to have replaced Elmer Hagar. To tell you the truth, this was a chance opportunity for me. I was set to take over as manager at Stillwell's dairy over in the next county, and I heard at the last minute that Elmer was leaving. I split my time between the animals and working here, but this is what I enjoy most."

"My father loves this place." Fuller let his eyes roam over the scene, the green grass spreading over the land, and the improvements that had changed the farm over the years.

"I hope to make your father see that this mill could well be profitable if he let me expand it. He's got a good source of wood, both on his land, as well as on the neighboring farms. I could make him rich with this mill alone."

"I don't think my father's interested in becoming rich. It provides a convenient source of raw lumber to be used on the farm." He diverted the remaining conversation from the mill. As he helped add wood to the firebox and restart the saw, he came to the conclusion that while Rex Kane displayed a cultured air in his use of words, his arrogant streak might be trouble for his father if he stayed overly long at Sweetwater.

At Rex's invitation, Fuller spent an enjoyable hour in manual labor at the saw mill, lifting the heavy logs and setting the band saw for the proper thicknesses of boards. He was careful of his hands, wearing thick leather gloves, for his hands were his treasure, whether holding a delicate scalpel, or stitching the flesh of a human body.

His father sent him to Johnie's house one afternoon to see about ordering a new belt for the band saw, and there, he hoped to reforge the brotherly relationship that had barely begun when he'd gone east to school. His brother was away, having taken the family's surrey into town to see the veterinarian there about some new and improved salve for the goats. One or two had jumped the fence, and Bevis, a farmer living about a mile away, had suggested he try something new the vet had recommended for his dog when it was bitten by a snake.

Vanessa, Johnie's wife, invited him in, offering him a glass of water. Pet was in the kitchen eating a cookie, and she pulled her plate close, using a finger to dab at crumbs scattered across the tabletop. Fuller could hear Rose, her sister, out back, her voice high and happy. It sounded as if she was calling to a dog. It was confirmed when Fuller heard the animal bark several times.

"I've been here a week, and I've barely seen you or the children." Fuller took the glass of water from his sister-in-law. "Your roses are beautiful. It's nice to see them inside, also."

"Johnie claims I do it for him." Vanessa reached to several blooms standing proudly in a clear vase at her side. "I have so many blossoms in the blooming season I hate to leave them all on the bush. Besides, they flower more profusely when I keep them thinned."

"It sounds as if you enjoy them as much or more than my brother." Fuller smiled as Vanessa reddened. "My lips are sealed. We'll let that brother of mine think it's all about him. You can let him know about the new belt. Papa said the old one's good for a time, but it might take several weeks or more to have another shipped out, if it has to come from the East Coast supplier. I'm afraid I'll be gone by then, and it'll be up to Johnie to see about it." He stood, and Vanessa took his glass.

As he approached the door, Pet came to her mother, throwing her arms around her and burying her face in her mother's dress. She patted her on her backside, sending her off to her room. "Fuller, thank you for coming by. I'll give Johnie the message."

"Perhaps someday you can tell me something of my brother's military escapades." Fuller hated to walk off too quickly. He'd probably never really know his brother's family, but he wished for more. "It might give me something to talk about with him. You do know I've considered a military career myself."

"I had no idea." By this time, Vanessa and Fuller were standing on the front porch, and they seated themselves on a wooden bench made from a split log turned rounded side down. "You're a successful surgeon. Why would you join the military?"

"You misunderstand me. I said I've considered it, not that I'd actually join. The idea of it, though, has some appeal."

"Not as much as you think."

Rose came out the front door, slamming the screen door back against the front wall of the house, and she crossed her arms with a pout. Her dog, a large, golden, short-haired mongrel followed her, standing at her feet and panting expectantly.

"What, dear?" Vanessa attempted to pull the child to her, but Rose stamped her foot, refusing to budge.

"Pet ate all the cookies. I didn't get any." Her eyes caught Fuller's face, and they narrowed, as if it was his fault.

"Honey, I offered one to you, and you wanted to play with Sargent."

"I told Pet to save me one. You heard me." Tears had begun to form in her eyes, and her bottom lip bulged outward.

"I know, sweetie. How about later I make up some more, and you can have the first one."

"Alright." Rose ran a hand through her hair, pulling it straight out from her head, and finally she leaned into her mother's hug, keeping her eyes on Fuller the entire time. "Can we make some now?"

"Your Uncle Fuller's here for a visit. When he's gone,

maybe." Vanessa brushed her daughter's hair from her face, and she kissed her cheek. "Will that do for you? Now, run inside, and tell Pet to help you set the table for supper. Don't forget, we need the big spoons out tonight. We're having stew."

Rose made a face, but she pulled away and slipped through the door. As soon as she was inside, she yelled, "I told you you were in trouble. Mama said I get all the cookies next time."

Vanessa shook her head and smiled at Fuller. "Were you and Johnie like that as children?"

"We were further apart in age. I didn't get to hear about my brother's army exploits, but it sounds like you have a meal to prepare. I'll get back to the mill and see how my father's doing. He's probably yelling at the saw, forcing it to make the proper cuts by force of his will, alone." He stood, pulling his heavy gloves on his hands.

Fuller slipped his hat on his head, and as he tugged the brim down, Vanessa turned and made her way into the house, calling out to Pet, "Did you eat all the cookies after I told you to save one for your sister?"

Fuller considered how fortunate his brother was. Vanessa was quite an attractive woman, with slender, beautiful hands, in spite of taking care of a busy household, and she had remained trim, also. If he ever married, he could definitely do worse. Maybe he would make a stronger attempt to bond with his brother. It seemed it would be the proper thing to do.

He spent more time with Janey and Walter and their children in the old station house, or in the inner garden on pleasant evenings in the softening shadows thrown onto the ground by the lateness of the hour.

"Heh, boys," he called to Franklin and Mark one sunny morning not long after the visit with Vanessa. He had no work anyone would let him do, and the boys seemed to be getting underfoot. He saw this as the perfect opportunity to get them out of everyone's hair. "I seem to remember a fish named Shimmer. That old fish has lived in the river since before I was born, so the stories say—"

"What stories, Uncle Fuller?" Mark interrupted, grabbing Fuller's arm and hanging on, while pulling his legs up to wrap them around one of Fuller's.

"Yeah, I don't remember no fish named Shimmer." Franklin darted around Fuller, poking at his brother. "Who told you that tale?" He was laughing, and when his brother tried to protect himself, he slipped and almost fell, except for Fuller making a quick grab.

"An old Indian I once knew used to tell me stories—"

"Indians? Weren't you scared?"

"Me? Never." Fuller grinned. It was clear he had the boys' attention. "His name was Standing Tree, and he could sing to the fish, and they'd come to the surface of the water, just begging for him to set a hook in their mouths."

"That's silly." Mark was trying to climb Fuller's arm again.

"It's true." Fuller nodded confidently, and he caught Franklin's eye, winking. Franklin was the bookish type, and he was certain the boy would find the tale intriguing, even if he wouldn't want to admit it might have actually happened.

The story of the fish named Shimmer went on long past the time they gathered up the fishing gear and made their way to the river. Old Shimmer didn't find his way to their hooks that morning, but there were several good-size trophies taken home for Janey to prepare for supper.

Later that evening, with the fish consumed and settling on their stomachs, Fuller held Gloria in his lap and read to her, creating a happy memory with his niece and her engaging laughter.

"Hey, sweet pumpkin. What story would you like tonight?"

"The one with the bears." She was dressed in a plaid frock with a low waist and black trim and buttons, her blonde hair in two braids that hung down in a wide circle and the ends tied behind her head with ribbons of red. She snuggled into his arms as she sorted through the three books in Fuller's hands. When she found the one she wanted, she offered it to him upside down.

Fuller opened it without righting it, and he began to read, "And Goldilocks woke up, and she screamed. She ran out the door and never saw the three bears again."

"No, Uncle Fuller. That's not right." She slapped at his arm. "Read the right words."

"I am." He pointed to the upside down picture of a little girl running out of a brown house with a red door. The words were at the top of the page, upside down, of course. "Now, if you want to start at the beginning, we might have to turn the book around."

Across the room Janey laughed softly, reaching to place her hand on her husband's arm. Walter looked at her, and she pointed to Gloria and Fuller, leaning in to whisper to him. Fuller could see her pantomiming turning a book upside down, and Walter smiled, pulling Janey's head to him and kissing her on the cheek. The baby, Noah, was cooing in a cradle at her feet, and she stepped gently on the curved runner nearest her and set it into a gentle motion.

Noah was already awake, however, and while barely able to walk, he could climb out of the cradle quite well. Before Janey could catch him, he was over the side, had stumbled over a wooden block and bellowed in anger and frustration. Walter picked him up and soothed his tears.

Fuller knew he would miss these times when he returned to California. Not enough to stay, but he would miss them nonetheless.

Fuller ordered his grandmother to the bedroom where he examined her and knew with a sinking heart that she hadn't long to live, her body worn out from the years of heavy toil of a farmer's wife and mother of three boys. He gave her some medicine to help with the pain in her hands and body, but he didn't think she would take it. He told no one of his diagnosis except Joe, and his father was saddened by the news, but had suspected the same himself.

He spent long evenings with his parents and heard again the old stories of their youth in Indiana and of their strange marriage day, and he could see the love in their eyes, one for the other.

Johnie stayed aloof, even with Fuller's attempts to break the ice, and Vanessa seemed to follow his lead. Fuller was surprised, after their talk on her front porch. The reason why soon became apparent, when she volunteered to mend a rent in his trousers he had gotten while working in the garden. Fuller was at the kitchen table nursing a glass of water, when Johnie came from the mill to confront him, his face red with pent-up emotion.

"Johnie, just talk to your brother. Tell him why you're so upset." Vanessa held the partially mended trousers in her hands, and she dropped them onto the table. "I cannot have you two at odds with each other, knowing you'll not be seeing each other for years. I just cannot."

"Brother?" Fuller felt the waste of the years gone, but this was his brother's issue and he couldn't resolve it on his own. He could see Johnie's eyes were red, and that was when Pet and Rose burst into the kitchen, Pet with a cookie in hand, and Rose hugging a curly-haired doll to her chest.

"Daddy?" Rose ran to her father and hugged his waist.

"Do we have anything to say, Johnie?" Fuller was prepared to leave, if the man didn't intend to mend the broken fence that always seemed to rear between them. His pants? He'd gladly dispose of them and purchase another pair.

"Well, it's like this." Johnie worked his lips, as if unable to get the words out. Then they vomited forth, "Janey cares about you more than me. I'm the one who's here. Janey always talks about you, like you're a hero, and I'm the one who was in the Army. All you do is eat fancy food out there in California, and it's not fair."

Ah, Janey, what have you done? Fuller knew he couldn't fix this in a day, or even a week, but Vanessa had given him some good advice on their previous visit.

"Brother, will you tell me something about one of your battles? The Indian wars, how about that? I'd enjoy hearing what you went through."

"Daddy, please?" Pet had finished her cookie, and she grabbed her daddy's arm.

"Johnie, for me?" Vanessa looked at him pensively, and she gave him a soft brush on the mouth with her lips.

Johnie looked away for a minute, then he smiled and looked at Fuller. "You really want to hear?"

"Of course I do." Fuller supposed his brother was doing it as much for the girls as for him, but they gathered in the living room, and as the tales unwound themselves from Johnie's memory, he found he was quite mesmerized. Darting through the forests, nighttime raids, and Indian guides from one tribe leading the Army in battles against rival tribes. With a smile at his wife, Johnie told of meeting her at Fort Riley in Kansas.

"I was afraid to talk to her, she was so beautiful, and she was the daughter of the commanding officer, as well." Fuller noted that when his brother said that, he looked truly in love.

"You weren't afraid. I remember that day I was in the sutler's store, and you offered to carry my packages for me." She smiled as she played with her daughter's hair.

"Offered?" Johnie laughed aloud. "You handed them to me, as if you didn't know who I was, just a convenient artillery man, handy to be your beast of burden."

"Oh, I knew, alright."

"And the next year I was transferred to Fort Sill."

"Oklahoma." Vanessa took a deep breath, clearly moved by the memory.

"And I thought I'd never see you again."

"But you did." She smiled, and the conversation continued to tell how her father had received a chance to also transfer into

Fort Sill, taking second in command, and he'd been reticent because of the Indian resettlements there in 1889. She'd worked for days to convince him it was the perfect posting.

"Then came the troubles with Geronimo and his Chiricahua. Fuller, you should've been there. He was fierce as I've ever seen, not like Standing Tree at all."

"You remember the old Indian?" Fuller laughed. "I thought he died when you were still a boy."

"Some, but Papa and Janey told me stories of him for years, making him into some sort of good-hearted shaman. I suppose I never understood the anger of the Indians until my army unit dealt with Geronimo. Even so, the man had to be contained, or people would die."

Fuller had never considered it, but he supposed his brother had achieved some level of respect in his military career. He wanted to be acknowledged for what he'd accomplished. The evening of storytelling was the beginning of that. He realized in his brother's stories that Standing Tree had become their pivot of connection, giving them a new understanding that had never been there before.

Thank God his father had accepted the Indian into life on the stage coach station. Even though the man was long dead, he was still doing what he'd always done, bringing people together and building family.

Later, as Johnie read to the girls from Vanessa's tattered leather copy of *Alice in Wonderland*, Vanessa whispered to Fuller that she knew all the stories about Standing Tree, but she'd never heard the story of the Indian guide during her husband's time in Oklahoma. She said she was glad Fuller and

Johnie were making up, and that she thought things would be different from then on. Fuller smiled at the prospect and enjoyed the story of the girl who fell down the rabbit hole as much as the girls did.

*****

Fuller had long since gotten over his attraction for Winnie Stafford and felt only a friendly fondness for her and her husband Tater. He admired their new son Randolph, called Randy, and crawled across the floor with him to the immense laughter of the rest of his family. He acquainted himself with the dogs that roamed the grounds and with the horses, mules and goats. He even milked the nannies a few times, feeling that he was taking part in the essential duties of the farm. There were three donkeys used for breeding, and he admired them, also. The boys liked to throw a noose around their necks and ride on their backs. It was innocent fun, and Joe didn't chastise them.

It was on the last night of his visit that he was taken aside by his father, and they spent the time talking of those things that concerned them both. They caught up on old friends that Joe had known from the days of yore. There weren't many left: Matthew Baldwin and his siblings, Hank Philips and Jim Owens, who continued to write occasionally of their families and life. Fuller had no clear plans, except to carry on his work. They spoke of politics and current events, and the prospect of war with Spain. They strolled around the perimeter of the grounds with a large mongrel dog Flop, named for how he flopped on the floor in front of the fireplace, his long ears flat against the brown boards. Joe would lean down and pat him on the head, and he would rise to be scratched or petted. He'd been a stray puppy who wandered onto the land, cold and with matted hair. Joe figured he'd been abandoned by his owners or lost in the woods.

The night was warm with a gentle breeze from the south, and Fuller could smell the pine and spruce of the forest as they walked. He drew his coat more closely to his chest; even in the summer, the cool higher atmosphere was chilling after sunset. The stars shone brightly overhead, and a quarter-moon hung loosely in the low eastern sky.

"Son, I've enjoyed your stay immensely. I know your mother and grandmother will miss you. Don't forget to write, and if you have need of funds, don't hesitate to let me know. What do I need of money, when I have everything I desire here? Next time you come, maybe you can bring Edward with you. He seems to be a fine young man and a good doctor. I've had several letters from him. I'll say my goodbyes now, for with all the hustle of departure in the morning, you'll be thinking of your trip." He took off his hat and scratched his head in the manner that Fuller had seen many times. "I don't often express my feelings, but I feel that with your present problems, I should say it. I love you. You were our first born, the fruit of our youth when the stages ran sporadically and the passengers were searching for a better future after the war. I'm proud of you and what you've become. Remember that when you feel lonely or troubled in that big city." Joe gave him a hug and took off in his bold stride for the house. He didn't look back, and Fuller felt the warmth of the hug for a long time as he continued to smoke a cigar and gaze at the far distant mountains, barely seen in the darkness, solid and compact against the night sky. He threw his smoke on the ground and used his heel to put out the flame. He went into the house, set out his clothes for the following day and slept peacefully though the night.

Fuller smelled bacon cooking as he rolled over in the bed. The perking of coffee drew him from sleep, and he knew he must get up and start the day. He had a long journey ahead of him and a full load of work waiting when he arrived. He took a quick bath, shaved his face and put away his things in his suitcase. He carried it and his medical bag down the stairs. The sight of his mother at the stove was familiar, and he moved to her and gave her a peck on her puckered cheek.

"Good morning, Mama. Did you sleep well?" He lifted a piece of bacon and took a bite. It was hot, and he gasped for air and swallowed quickly.

Hannah laughed. "Well enough. Have you got everything packed? Did you remember to put the new shirt in your bag? Walter's decided to drive you. Tater has to tend to a mule that knocked down the top log on the fence and has a scratch on his leg. Those stupid mules, always trying to escape into the forest." She set a cup on the table and poured the hot, fragrant liquid from the pot into it, her exasperation showing in her actions.

"Yes, everything's packed neatly, and I remembered the new shirt. Thank you. One more shirt is always welcome." He put the rest of the bacon in his mouth and chewed. He turned when he heard a sound at the door.

Joe stepped into the room, followed by Flop and the smaller

dog Grover, named for a stage guard of long ago. They trotted to the stove and begged for food, drool dropping onto the floor. Joe looked tired; his hair was uncombed and his face unshaven. His chest was bare, and he held his shirt in his hand. Even with modern facilities, he still did his shaving in the kitchen, where the water was hot, and the smell of food permeated the room.

"Good morning, son. Darling, that smells good." He kissed her, and she laughed. "What? Is something funny?" He was now wide awake. He dipped hot water into a bowl, placed his shaving kit on the table and hung his shirt over a chair. He glanced around.

"I was just thinking of Standing Tree coming in of a morning, his blanket wrapped tightly around him. And Jack, on the floor beside the stove begging for food." The two men looked at the dogs, and they laughed, too.

"What made you think of Standing Tree this morning?" Joe started to lather his chin and looked at her with an odd smile.

"Oh, I think it was the last few days, all this talk of old times, when Fuller was small and the rush to get the passengers up and on the road. Do you remember how Rusty would growl and curse when he tried to get the women to hurry so he could keep to his schedule? And Grover, so stiff and solemn holding the mail bag in his hand." She turned to Fuller, while Joe continued with his shaving.

"Rusty was our first driver; he brought us from Mozier Station, with Scrappy beside him." She stopped to pour Joe a cup of coffee. Fuller sipped his coffee and waited. She refilled his cup. He was glad that she was talking of the old days; he knew it was her way of keeping back the tears. "The road crew was working in the forest, and there was the sound of sawing and trees falling as the stage stopped under the cottonwoods and willows. I was the only woman within twenty-five miles. Do you remember, Joe?" In spite of her best efforts, she had to stop and lift her apron to wipe the tears.

"Oh, botheration. I promised myself I'd be strong and brave, but I can't help it. I'll miss you, son. It'll be like watching the coaches again, passing from sight and the silence closing down on the station. I think that's why your papa chopped so much wood. He couldn't stand the silence."

Joe had finished and wiped his face dry, and he donned his shirt. He buttoned it while he crossed to the table. "You might be right, dear. I've chopped a few logs in the last years. Mmmmm. Better get those biscuits out of the oven before they burn."

"Ah, damn." If the men in her life were surprised at the curse, they didn't say as Hannah picked up a thick cloth and opened the oven door. She drew out a long, flat pan, grown black from many years of usage, full of hot, brown sweet rolls. She put them on the stove and closed the door.

Fuller turned at the sound of the door, and Winnie Stafford stood there holding the baby in her arms. She put him in the tall chair beside the table and proceeded without a word to help Hannah with breakfast. They began to wander in, first his grandmother, then Janey and her children, and Johnie and Vanessa and their daughters. The chatter of family conversation as they ate and shuffled their feet or laughed drove away all thoughts or mention of the old days as preparations got underway for Fuller's departure.

As Fuller moved his things to the porch, he saw the hired hand Jake hanging around the corral with a straw between his lips, wearing muddy boots and the hem of his trousers caked in grime, as though he'd been watering the animals. He looked at the wagon near the house, then at Fuller, and he nodded. Fuller remembered a book he'd finished, and he wondered if the boy enjoyed reading. He worked it out of his bag and made his way that direction.

"Jake, how's that calf coming along? Any more bloat?"

"Nah, been doing fine. You about off, Doc?" He leaned against the corral and twisted at the straw in his mouth.

"Got something for you. I finished this book the other day, and I don't really have room to carry it back. Thought you might like it." He held it up.

"To read?" Jake glanced at Joe coming out of the house and back at Fuller. "No one ever gave me a book before. What's it about?"

"You'll enjoy it. *The Celebrated Jumping Frog of Calaveras County,* filled with funny stories. Here." He held the book out.

Jake took it, opening the book and turning a few pages. He looked up grinning, and he scratched his head. "This is great, Doc. I don't read too well, but I'll sure read this." He dug his boot into the soil, and he looked pleased.

Fuller walked away smiling, gratified to have made the boy so happy. Back across the yard, he lifted his bags into the flatbed wagon, gave everyone a hug or handshake and jumped into the passenger seat of the surrey as Bub drove away on the forest road to Denver. They arrived in plenty of time for him to board the train. He told Walter not to wait, and they shook hands. He watched his old friend walk away and waved at Jake who had driven the wagon. He found a vendor and bought a newspaper and some magazines to while away the time. His mind drifted back to the morning, and he had a premonition that he would never see his grandmother again. He felt the sting of bitter tears and blinked them away. He studied the headlines of the paper but couldn't see the words, his mind still full of the last few days. He rose and walked around to relieve the tension, and by the time his train was called, Fuller was thinking of his profession and San Francisco once more.

Eleven

Fuller took a hansom cab to his home and office and arrived shortly before noon. He paid the driver and lifted his luggage from the back seat. He unlocked the front door and walked in to the sound of raised voices.

A bald, portly man in the clothes of a dock worker was yelling at Edward, who stood tense and stiff, doing some cursing of his own.

"What's the trouble?" Both men turned at the sound of the voice and started to talk at the same time. Fuller held up his hand. The stevedore turned, his face red and damp with sweat.

"What's it to you?" He held his cap in his hand and his hands looked rough and brown.

"I'm Dr. Hadley. I live and work here." He indicated his medical bag and valise that he had just put on the floor. He placed his keys back in his pocket.

"You're Dr. Hadley? Thought you were an older man." He looked at Ed and back to Fuller, then trying to calm himself, he burst out with his complaint.

"This young man who calls hisself a doctor, says I got to pay my bill, even though the baby died. Said it makes no difference whether the child lives or not, the wife used his services during the birthing. I says, he didn't save the baby, so it don't count. I said I'd pay him for the birth of my wife's child, but I ain't got no child." He huffed and blew out his cheeks, and Fuller was impressed.

He turned to Ed. "What do you say, doctor?" he asked formally, hoping to calm the muddy waters of the argument.

"Fuller, you know we can't afford to help everyone who needs it for free. I tried to tell Mr. Sadler that, but he insists that he doesn't owe us for my services since the baby died."

"Did your wife survive, Mr. Sadler? Is she well?"

"Yes, the doc says she'll be fine in a few days and can have more children if we're blessed by the good Lord."

"Well, there's your answer. Dr. Murray agreed to attend your wife during her travail, and he apparently carried out his duties. He should be paid for his services."

"I should have known. The two of you don't understand. I don't have no baby. I paid for the delivery of a baby, and he died." He began to huff out his cheeks again, and Fuller watched, fascinated.

"Where do you work, Mr. Sadler? On the docks? Do you get paid regular wages for your work?"

The man looked at Fuller as though he had questioned his integrity. He cursed.

"Of course, I get paid regular. We have a contract with the company. If'n we didn't get paid, we'd quit."

117

"Since you get paid for your work, then why do you think that Dr. Murray shouldn't get paid for his? Is that fair? You said your wife is healthy and able to birth more children, so our responsibility to you is finished. We have a contract, too. Didn't you sign your name giving the doctor permission to attend your wife?" He took his hat from his head and began to remove his gloves. He placed the gloves inside the hat and rested them on the table beside the door, while the man was thinking it through.

Suddenly, it was like a bright light shone on the antagonist's face. "Damn, if you ain't right. I did make my mark on the paper, and I agreed to pay the charges. Dr. Hadley, you're a smart man. But, I don't have the cash until the first of the month when we get paid. Can you wait until then?" and he looked first at Fuller then at Ed with hopefulness.

"Yes, we'll wait for the payment, and no hard feelings, sir." Ed brought himself back into the conversation.

Mr. Sadler broke into a smile and shook hands with each of the men, stuffed his soft cap on his head and sailed from the room like one of the whaling schooners at the docks.

Fuller turned when he heard a sound just beyond the parlor door. Galena Fairchild came from the room, laughing.

"Lordy, doctor, you'd charm the snake in the Garden of Eden into eating that apple instead of Eve and Adam. I never saw such smooth talk in all my days. It was a pleasure to hear it."

"Just be sure to mark down the payment when it arrives. My experience comes from my father who was the manager of a relay stage station until the railroads started running through the area. He dwelt with all kinds of situations in his time. I think I picked up a thing or two watching him." Fuller hefted his luggage and started for the stairs. "Give me a few minutes to unpack and freshen up, and I'll be with you." He paused for a response, and receiving none, he climbed the stairs to his room.

Inside his room, he threw his bag on the bed and removed the contents, putting his undergarments and dirty shirts in the basket that held such items until Fanny did the washing. He hung his suit on a peg near the door so it would air out. He hoped it wouldn't have to be cleaned, for that was additional expense out of his meager funds. He took fresh clothing and his shaving kit to the water closet. Opening the kit, he laid out his silver-handled brush, a slightly stained shoe horn, his tooth brush and tooth powder, one straight razor and several silver-topped bottles of cologne. He chose one and twisted the top, sniffing before deciding on another with a spicy-citrus aroma. He set it aside to use once he was dressed. He placed a round cake of woody-scented soap near the tub. Lathering his face, he gave his straight razor several fast rubs against the strop to ensure it was sharpened, and pressed it repeatedly to his neck and jaw. Wiping the remaining lather with a cloth, he bathed and dressed for office hours. He sighed as he left his room and went back downstairs for his dinner. His vacation time was over, and he greeted his partner and Fanny with a smile.

After all the patients had left and Galena had cleaned the surgery and sterilized the used instruments, the two men sat in the office to discuss the medical cases involved and to catch up on what had happened in his absence.

"I can't thank you enough, Fuller, for getting me out of that argument. I would have put it down as a charity case, had I not

known that he got paid regularly. Besides, we need the money."
He laughed. "I agree with Galena, you're good with the people.
I can do the healing and the pill dispensing, but I hate to talk to
the people. We make a good team."

"I think so, too. I'm grateful that you asked me to come to
San Francisco to start my medical practice. I figure a few more
months, and the instruments will be paid for, and we can expand
with more equipment. Tell me, are you still seeing Grace? Is
she as pretty as when I left?" He grinned.

"No, I overheard some men at the hospital, and they said
she was hoping for a marriage proposal, so I told her we didn't
suit, and she started walking out with Clark Hewett. I wish them
well. I met a new girl Friday night at the dancing hall when I
went with a few of the men from pediatrics." He held up his
hand. "I know what you're going to say, we can't afford that
place, but how're we going to get ahead if we hang around the
slums and the tenements? We need contacts with rich patients
and their society friends if we're going to survive." And he
laughed until Fuller smiled at him, for he felt the same. He
would continue to work with the poor, but he had plans for his
own life, and it didn't include this rambling old house with the
creaking floors and grumbling water pipes.

Twelve

Fuller plunged into the lifestyle of a young, single doctor; working long hours during most of the week, but taking advantage of the entertainments available and that he could afford in his leisure time. The year seemed to slip by with rapid speed. Rumors of war mounted, and when, shortly after the Christmas season wound down, the newspapers carried pictures of the tragic sinking of one of the Navy's sea-going coast-line battleships in Havana harbor, Fuller brought the matter to Ed's attention in no uncertain way.

"Ed, my man," Fuller exclaimed, as he tossed a folded newspaper on the table in their common dining room. "Have you seen this?" He was incensed. He recalled the occasional stories of his father's war years, and hearing him speak with men coming through on the stage lines about how the past needed to be put aside so men could move forward in their lives. Now the Spanish government had the nerve to order one of America's three premier ships, the only ones of their kind in existence, to be sunk. It amounted to sedition against America, much less considering the lives that were surely lost when the vessel went down.

"Eh? What is this?" Ed pulled up the paper to lay it flat. He was in a white shirt underneath suspenders, with his sleeves unbuttoned and rolled, and his hair was in disarray on one side. A cigar smoldered off to the side, the end in a ceramic saucer, and a healthy pile of ash filling up the center. He reached for it, tapped it absently, and took a draw before blowing smoke into the room, aiming it at the ceiling as he perused the images on the front page.

"That!" Fuller thumped the picture of the *USS Maine*, aflame, surrounded by smaller firefighting vessels that were valiantly attempting to subvert the flames to rescue the ship. The massive guns off her bow were pointed near skyward, and the conning tower arched into the sky. The U.S. standard flew overhead, red, white and blue against a deepening sky, caught by the camera's lens snapping in a stiff breeze. The flames were so bright they lighted the surroundings like midday.

"My word, man, is that one of ours?" Ed sat up, dropping his cigar into the saucer and drawing the paper closer. He traced the words under the picture with his finger, as if in disbelief at what they said.

"The *Maine*. Don't you recognize it? Sunk at near ten at night. I hear over 250 men possibly went down with her. How could Spain do such a thing?"

"Are we to declare war?" Ed turned the page to continue the story on the inside of the paper. There were more pictures, several showing injured sailors being pulled from the waters, their faces harsh in the glare of flashbulbs, with some dressed only in their navy-issued skivvies. A number sported serious burns. Other pictures were evidently taken the following morning, revealing twisted parts of the warship's superstructure piercing the water's surface. Small boats bobbed on the surface, examining the decimated remains of what had once been one of the flagships of America's naval fleet.

"The *Oregon* is already under orders to return to the city. San Francisco's her home port." By this time, he'd calmed down, and he pulled a chair out and reached across the table to take Ed's cigar in his hand, pulling a deep draw from the end. "You remember, Eddie, when we went to the wharfs last year and admired the massive vessel in the harbor?"

"I'm admiring my cigar about now." Ed tapped his fingertips on the table, his eyes intent on his cigar in Fuller's hand.

Fuller laughed. "I believe the *Oregon* might need fresh medical officers on board. If I volunteer, do you suppose I might receive a field commission?"

"Are you a fool?" Ed closed the paper and slapped it down flat, making an awful sound. "We have a fine practice here, you and me. How will I make the clinic function without you?"

"You're a fine example of American patriotism. See it a different way. This might be the start of a grand adventure. Discover more of the world." Fuller smiled, and he reached to pull on Ed's suspenders, releasing them to pop against his chest.

"Oh, says the world traveler. I'm quite content. If I should choose to head out, I suspect Alaska's more my calling. What say you, how does that sound to the other half of my medical practice?" Ed pushed his chair away, scraping the legs loudly before standing. He held the saucer of ashes out, waiting until Fuller dropped the cigar butt on it, before dispensing the smoking ember into a covered metal container to allow it to die and cool before a more permanent disposal.

Fuller laughed loudly, leaning back in his chair. "Alaska! There's no war in Alaska. We'll see. Perhaps nothing will come of this." He pulled the paper to him, studying the image of the *Maine*. "Then, just maybe I'll get my sea legs back, and I'll travel the world once more."

*****

Fuller devoured the newspapers, and when he read that the government called for young, healthy medical workers, he visited a recruiter and signed up for the duration. He gave his qualifications as a graduate of a prestigious Eastern school, and touted his practice at St. Michael's as a surgeon. He was quite fastidious, he assured the recruiters, and being unmarried, there was nothing to keep him in San Francisco. He was promised his services would be appreciated somewhere, perhaps in the expected conflagrations that would arise in the Pacific if the upcoming head-to-head with Spain became an international incident as was expected. There was some thought that Guam and perhaps the Philippines might become embroiled in the conflict, and who knew, Hawaii had been petitioning for U.S. annexation since '93. The recruiters couldn't make a judgment, but anything was possible with the tensions strung so high.

Fuller noticed the word war was never mentioned, but he supposed it would come to that. The destruction of the *Maine* said as much. He wrote to his father to explain his decision and received a reply that Joe and Hannah were proud of him. But, the letter included tragic news, too, for his grandmother, Ruth, had died in her sleep the week before.

He grieved for a time, but he knew that she was free of the pain and crippling disease she had suffered most of her adult life. He could imagine the place of her burial beside her husband among the tall pines and fragrant spruce trees of Sweetwater Springs. He sent a long letter of condolences and prepared for his departure for service in the medical corps of the United States Navy. In this he felt a bond with his younger brother, Johnie, who had served during the Indian war years, and his father, who had fought in the Civil War. This would be a new kind of war, battles fought in a far land, and he would be treating the wounded and dying, instead of carrying a rifle in his hands.

Fuller spent several mornings at the wharfs, viewing the goings on. The *USS Oregon* was in port by then, loading ammunition, supplies, and coal. He and Edward Murray parted company, their debts paid and their friendship intact. Ed would be leaving for Alaska, as he'd suggested, where gold had been discovered; he hoped to strike it rich, but if not, his skill and experience as a physician would be needed. The house was sold at a fine profit, and the money divided equally between them. Fuller's personal items were boxed and shipped to Colorado to be stored until his return. Galena and Fanny were provided a small pension for their services, and both were still young enough to find other employers. A trio of fresh-faced and eager doctors, straight from their residencies at the local medical school, settled into the practice, and Fuller was satisfied that the work with the poor and homeless would continue.

Fuller moved into the Palace Hotel, but only until he received his assignment papers. He whooped for joy to discover he was, indeed, to be aboard the *Oregon* as assistant physician. She hoped to sail on March 19. He learned he would share responsibility for over 30 officers, 400 enlisted men, and a company of 60 marines. He was given a week to become accustomed to the layout of the ship.

One of Fuller's prized items to move aboard the ship was a new Sanderson camera, along with a supply of sheet film to ensure numerous photo opportunities. It had a tripod and a folding accordion-type front. If he was to see the entire South American continent, he wanted a record of the places he visited. His first picture was of the *Oregon* as she sat moored in port. For his second, he stood in front of the camera, and using a remote attachment on a long cable, snapped an image of himself in front of the battleship.

The first few days out from port were uneventful, with Fuller getting to know some of the men. There were more than he could keep track of at first, but the captain, Charles Clark, who had replaced Capt. A. H. McCormick on the day before their departure, announced right off that their orders were to make it to Florida at utmost speed. Their first stop would be Callao, Peru, to re-coal the bunkers and await further orders.

A young navy seaman named Enrico Rodriguez was assigned to Fuller as an orderly to facilitate his duties onboard the vessel.

"Hey, there, Rodriguez, sort those linens in the wardrobe

and give me a final count." This was one of the chores Fuller hadn't been able to get to over the course of the previous week. He'd concentrated on medical supplies, but now he needed desperately to know how well stocked he was for the necessary sanitary needs of a complement of nearly 500 men, should a number of them fall ill concurrently. Shipboard laundry facilities weren't his, alone, to commandeer.

The dark-haired sailor, with his deep-toned skin and black eyes, mumbled something in Spanish, causing Fuller to look at him with a frown.

"How is that, Rodriguez?" Fuller knew some very basic Spanish. Not enough to converse but he'd caught a few words. *Mucho*. Much. *Muerte*. Death.

"My apologies, sir. My family speaks Spanish for my grandfather, and I forget, sometimes." Enrico smiled and shrugged.

"Perfectly understandable. You said something about much death. What's that about?" Fuller set his record-keeping pad aside, adjusting his pencil carefully so it wouldn't roll to the floor if the ship hit a rough patch in the sea. He waited patiently on the younger man.

"I see the signs coming, as do many people. You must know, I'm Spanish, but of course, not full blood, not with my Indian grandmother." The man smiled and touched his cheek, as if to indicate his richly-colored skin.

"That's perfectly alright. You're also American, I presume?" He would have to be, or he wouldn't be onboard the *Oregon*.

"Yes, sir. My great-grandfather wasn't. He came to

California from Spain to claim his land, and we've lived here since that time." He was counting as he talked, and he marked a tally of his first stack on a paper in his hand.

"Ah, a Spanish land grant, probably from the king? Was your great-grandfather an aristocrat?" Fuller wanted to smile, but he refrained. Rodriguez was being so serious that he didn't think it suitable. Still, it was so different from his own upbringing on the edges of the Colorado mountains. He wondered how his father would respond to know that his son was hobnobbing with Spanish royalty. Well, almost royalty, anyway.

"In Spain, yes, and here, also. My family still resides in the hacienda constructed by my great-grandfather."

"What year did he arrive?" Fuller knew enough of his history to suspect they'd been there upwards of a hundred years.

"My father takes pride in telling everyone he knows of the year." Enrico laughed, his face lighting up for the first time. "It's marked on his grant, signed by the great King Charles in 1803. That was long before I was born, so I just say a very long time ago."

"Now, what was that about death?"

"If there's war, there'll be much death, I think."

Fuller agreed as they continued to count the linens in the wardrobe. Their tally sheets completed, he filled out the proper forms and tossed them on the stack of other papers.

*****

Before the ship reached Peru, Fuller found out something his young orderly excelled at. Some of the men had experienced severe bouts of seasickness. He had several cases of Whelpton's Headache, Purifying Sea Sickness pills onboard, but found they only assuaged some of the symptoms. One of the men, Petty Officer Gilroy, became dehydrated, and during the night, Fuller heard a guitar through his cabin wall.

"What the hell," he muttered, climbing out of bed and pulling on a robe. He pushed the door ajar to find Rodriguez softly strumming a guitar and singing to the sick man in Spanish.

"Ah, sir." Enrico pressed his hand against the strings, and the instrument went silent. "I didn't mean to wake you. The man said his mother used to sing him to sleep when he was a boy, and I hoped I'd have some success. Mi madre used to do the same for me."

"Shh." Fuller put his finger to his lips. "It seems to have worked." Sure enough, Gilroy's eyes were closed, and he was snoring quietly. He motioned for the orderly to exit the room with him, and Fuller closed the door, being careful to latch it with as little noise as possible.

Gilroy had to be put ashore at Callao, where hopefully he would recover and be able to reboard a Navy vessel the next time it entered port. It turned out he had more than seasickness. He had an undisclosed ear perforation that he'd dealt with from a child, and he was afraid he'd be refused his service if he was discovered. He'd been in a public bath just before the *Oregon* sailed, and he'd opened himself up to an infection that Fuller didn't have the equipment to deal with on the ship. Fuller assured the man he'd receive adequate care while in Peru, and he'd file a report recommending the man for further military action should the conflict with Spain continue on through the summer.

Fuller was obligated to accompany Gilroy to the local hospital while the ship was being resupplied and stocked with coal, but the enlisted men stayed aboard. Re-coaling the bunkers would take more than a day, but they dared not risk the ship's contingent getting drunk and missing the upcoming departure. Fuller thought it just as well, because he'd carried his camera with him, hoping to find something significant in the city to expose a frame of film. He met a charming nurse at the hospital just going off duty, and he invited her for a cup of coffee at a local diner. She spoke no English, but they seemed to get along just fine in spite of it, and he captured her beauty in three distinct portrait shots, with views of the distant harbor in the background. Later, he considered he might have learned more about the dark-haired filly if Rodriguez had accompanied him, but then, he'd enjoyed the brief interlude from his ship-board duties.

They steamed away on April 7. It had been nearly three weeks, and they'd barely started on their voyage. News about the war was intermittent. However, at the Straits of Magellan, they anchored at Port Tamar, as a severe storm had borne down upon them, and they were afraid to continue on. Fuller was given the opportunity to administer more of Whelpton's remedy for seasickness, although every man seemed to recover this time, each with some measure of good response to the medication. That decided him that Gilroy's continued debilitation had been undue to seasickness in the first place, and that Whelpton's was rather a good remedy to have on hand.

That was the night the ship was thought to be on fire, as a smell of burning cloth and scorched flesh filled the corridors, setting off a fire alarm. At the first sound of the klaxon, Fuller dropped a bottle of iodine he was administering to a minor cut, and it stained a large area on the floor. Rodriguez claimed he could remove it easily, but Fuller was certain it would still be there after much scrubbing. A good portion of the ship began to fill with smoke. Fuller made his way into the haze of the corridor, only to be sent back inside his quarters and told he would be in the way. Before the lifeboats could be manned, the alarm was cancelled. It was only later Fuller learned that a coal bunker next to a magazine store had ignited, but the ship's firemen were experienced, and it was extinguished handily. In the melee, the meat cooking for the evening meal was overlooked, and it was thoroughly burnt, bringing the scuttle-butt the next day that the cook was determined to poison every-one aboard. It was tossed overboard, and the crew had sand-wiches for the evening meal. It was a long several hours putting salve on several burned hands, but the men expressed their gratitude for his help, and everyone seemed to be on the road to recovery.

The next day they made Puntas Arenas to re-coal the bunkers yet again, leaving in three days' time accompanied by the gunboat Marietta. Word passed through the ship that the United States had finally declared war on Spain. Fuller and Rodriguez were topside, taking in the sea air, and Fuller was glad to see the Marietta steaming along at their side as an assurance that they would make it safely to Florida. He stood at the railing, watching the waves crossing its bow. Up and down the ship, men were going about their duties. Black smoke billowed from the single stack, and its standard whipped briskly, suspended from the top of the mast. Lifeboats hung from the side, extended over the water, and Fuller hoped they wouldn't need to be put into use. Whether the entire contingent of the ship could make it to safety in the smaller vessels got him to thinking about his own ship, and he shivered at the ramifications.

Clouds began to move in and soon obscured the horizon. The Marietta hit a patch of fog, disappearing for a moment, her lights barely visible. It looked as if rain would come before the next dawn, and the assistant surgeon and his orderly wanted to catch fresh air while they could. Fuller noted that Rodriguez was in a despondent mood after hearing of the Declaration of War, and he questioned him on the matter.

"Alright, Rodriguez, I can see you're having a time of it. What's with the long face?"

"It's nothing, sir. A private matter." Rodriguez had a foot up on the lower railing, and his arms rested on the top support. He looked out to sea, but his face remained morose. The wind had turned cool, and rain started to spatter the water.

"I'm here if you need to talk." Fuller hunched his jacket up as he leaned on the railing in a similar fashion to encourage the conversation to develop.

"My cousin, sir. He spent several years with me at my family's hacienda when we were young men. Now this talk of war. It drives even families apart, you know, and that's not right."

"Is he serving in the military, too?"

"The Spanish military, the navy, to be precise." Rodriguez stood up and ran his hands through his hair. "You see, now? He returned to Spain when he was fifteen. Now I'm worried that we might have to face one another in battle."

"And you don't know if you can do it, to kill one of your own. Picture it from your cousin's viewpoint. How would he see it?"

That made Rodriguez laugh. "My cousin would have no such qualms. He'd shoot first, then wire his mother in Spain and say his American cousin is dead like the dog he is."

Fuller laughed, and he promised he wouldn't share that story. He suggested Rodriguez not repeat it, either, and Rodriguez agreed it wouldn't be a good idea.

At Rio de Janeiro, in Brazil, they planned a longer stop, and with the extended time aboard ship, the men were given leave for short periods. As war had already been declared with Spain, tensions on all sides were high, but Rodriguez was a boon to the *Oregon*, Capt. Clark exclaimed, when he found the man spoke some Portuguese as well as fluent Spanish. "Someone to speak Spanish fluently, that I expected, but Portuguese, also! My God, you are the best thing that has happened to me aboard ship. I'm honored to have you as part of my crew, sailor. I should leave Dr. Hadley in Rio and promote you to my personal assistant." He laughed when he said it to show he meant it as a compliment, not as a serious consideration, and went toward the bow and gazed at the city in the distance.

After leaving Rio, at Bahia Salvador, Brazil, they received a warning of a Spanish fleet nearby, so they steamed away the next day, re-coaling the bunkers in Bridgetown, Barbados, a week and a half later. While in the island port, Fuller stood on deck, having a leisurely smoke, listening to the casual talk of the sailors as they moved about. Fuller was especially caught by the scent of flowers wafting in off the shore. There was a ship nearby that must have been filled with spices, because when the wind shifted, he could smell cinnamon and other alluring aromas that made him remember his mother's sweet rolls from his childhood home at the Sweetwater Station in Colorado. After a time, however, he was touched on the shoulder by Rodriguez. He was needed below to re-bandage a sailor's wound received when he'd injured his leg during the storm off the coast of Argentina, and it had refused to heal properly.

They finally anchored near Jupiter Inlet, Florida, and Fuller was glad to be back to American waters. On May 26, the *Oregon* arrived in Key West and received orders to the nearest U.S. Naval Station or, if possible, to join the North Atlantic Fleet.

Corporal Weston Whatley, a Marine Fuller had treated for seasickness and had grown to enjoy his company, sat in the physician's quarters with a game of checkers between them. Fuller was red, and Whatley was playing the black. Fuller had crowned three of his pieces, and Whatley was struggling to stay afloat.

"Ah, Doc, there's no way to win against you." Whatley ran a hand through his hair, which was about due for the ship's barber, and he moaned with exaggerated despair. "If I play any of the obvious moves, you'll take me down like dominoes stacked in a row."

"The way the game's designed." Fuller smiled. He played the same moves every time, but the man didn't seem to see how he did it. Much like the Spanish, he mused. They were in a losing position in this war they'd drawn America into, and they didn't seem to understand how the United States managed to be successful against all comers.

"Here, this piece might work. If I play it here . . ." Whatley touched one of his pieces, pale finger on black wood, and he paused, his eyes searching for possible flaws in his play. "Alright, here we go." Before he could lift his hand, the ship lurched, and the entire board slipped. The pieces on the board shifted sideways a half inch as if in a coordinated dance. The ship shivered again as it settled into the water. Whatley lifted his finger and laughed, saying, "Glad I had my finger there. We would've lost the entire board."

"I thank you, sir, and Spain is going down." Fuller laughed and jumped the man six times, effectively ending the game. News had already reached them about Commodore George Dewey's magnificent defeat of the Spanish fleet in Manila Bay on the first of May. Only seven U.S. seamen had received injuries, and Fuller assumed the casualties on the other side had been quite high. He gathered up the confiscated game pieces one at a time, stacking them on his side of the board.

"How do you do that, and every time?" Whatley didn't sound overly upset, and he stood and looked out a small port hole in one wall of the room. It was opened, as summer had broached southern Florida in full force. A sea breeze wafted in, carrying the smell of the ocean tainted with oil, coal smoke and overheated metal. It offered a cooling touch, but the room was stifling, nonetheless. Whatley was in his undershirt, and the back was damp with sweat.

"When do you think we'll engage the enemy?"

"The Spanish, you mean?" Sounds of orders being given and the clanking of metal against the exterior of the ship filtered inside, an ominous accompaniment to the question that hadn't yet been answered.

"You, being the military man, must have some idea of what's about to happen." Fuller prodded the sailor.

"We cast off to join the North Atlantic Fleet in the morning." Whatley turned to look at Fuller. "If someone asks, you didn't hear it from me."

"Ah, with Admiral Sampson."

"Where did you learn that?" Whatley moved with surprising speed to the table, and he dropped into the chair, with his arms crossed before him, leaning in to look Fuller in the eye. "You're not to know that. No one is."

"Even you?" Fuller smiled, pleased at his coup of information. He'd picked up the tidbit while tending to a seaman in the weapon stores who had cut his arm on a sharp piece of metal and needed it sewn up and bandaged. Two officers had been discussing upcoming orders, and Fuller had been invisible to them.

"Own up, Doc. Where'd you get that little jewel?"

Fuller drew a finger across his mouth and shook his head, standing and gathering up the game pieces. Whatley got his signal, and he pulled his shirt off Fuller's bed, slipped it on and waved good night before slipping out the door.

136

The tension aboard the *Oregon* was tight, with nerves stretched to breaking points and beyond. Upon joining the North American Fleet, they had been greeted with cheers and shouts of approval. They were now with the fleet nearing Cuba, but the men aboard ship seemed to expect to come upon a mine with every mile of water covered. Fuller made his way to the deck one night to smoke, hiding his match as he struck it against its case, only to see the lights of an oncoming ship. He ducked behind a pole, as his heart thumped wildly in his chest to think it might be one of the enemy. It turned out to be a messenger boat, coming from the *USS New York*, Admiral Sampson's armored cruiser.

Watching the messenger boat pull alongside, and the sailors aboard clambering to the deck of the *Oregon*, Fuller remembered the picture of the *Maine*, with flames flaring and men being pulled from the water with burns covering their arms and legs. He'd had Rodriguez prepping his medicinal supplies so the necessary medicines for treating war wounds were easily accessed. He might very well need them all, and when he needed them he would need them quickly. He headed down to his quarters after snuffing out his smoke. He stood in the darkness for a few moments lighted only by the corridor lamps filtering in through his open door when a man called to him.

"Sir, you in there?"

The voice was Rodriguez's, and Fuller called out, "In here, sailor. What can I do for you?" He was at the small porthole watching the ships at their side and the water trailing along behind them as they steamed forward. He didn't turn, but he heard the man come in.

"Life jacket." Something soft fell on the bed. "Just in case there's mines. I don't want you to go under if we go down."

Fuller appreciated the man's consideration. "We're to be on blockade duty. We won't enter the harbor." That much had come down the pipe.

"Yes, sir."

"Thank you, Rodriguez. I'm off to bed. Get yourself a good night's sleep. Close the door on the way out."

"Yes, sir." The door clicked shut, and Fuller was alone.

It was ten-thirty when a general call went up, pulling Fuller from his bed. He yawned, rubbing his eyes, when the ship shuddered. He pulled on his pants and made his way to the corridor to learn a torpedo boat was sighted and engaged. The incident happened and was over before he was able to find out any details.

Two days later, the ship's guns fired repeatedly, as the *Oregon* and her sister ships bombarded Spanish fortifications on the island. Fuller thought he might go insane himself, if the booming didn't stop soon. Finally, things were quiet, and for a week after that, searchlights blared from the ship, looking for any possible enemy ships that might be in the water. As the days of summer rolled around, Fuller thought he might have some time to organize his supplies, as the ship's coal stores were running low, and she made her way to Guantanamo for re-coaling. It didn't go as he planned. Men were in and out of Fuller's surgery, mostly with stress concerns, headaches and the like. There was a concern with malaria, but with the constant wind from the sea breezes, the ship's contingent of men hadn't faced much of a problem.

All hell broke loose on the third of July as the fleet fired on the Spanish ships at Santiago. The *Oregon* remained offshore, but Fuller had his porthole barricaded against the smoke filling the air. In the occasional lull, using a small spy glass, he could see in the distance that things weren't going well for the Spanish ships. Many had decks of wood construction, and as shells struck they splintered, and he could see men and shattered parts of the ships flying through the air. Flames spread across the water, as burning oil overtook those who had jumped from the Spanish ships to the perceived safety of the island waters. A lifesaving ring soared high and white through the sky, silhouetted boldly against the blackening smoke billowing from a crippled ship, landing near one man. A partially visible life boat from another ship pulled the floundering man to safety. Sometime later, Fuller was called to the surgery to find the man pulled from the sea awaiting him there.

"Do you speak English, man?" He scrubbed his hands and arms as he prepared to offer his medical expertise to one of the enemy. He pushed that thought away. He was helping an injured man, and that's what he must keep in mind.

"No hablo Inglés. Español, por favor." The man moaned. He was severely burned, and he was bleeding through his drenched clothing. One hand was wrapped in blood-soaked rags, and his head was painted red down the side.

"Rodriguez!" Fuller took a large scissors and cut the shirt off the man to discover the cause of the blood. His side had been skewered by a ragged fragment of shrapnel. It seemed to be the only thing holding the man's organs inside his body.

"Sir?" Rodriguez leaned inside, and he paled at the sight of the blood now dripping to the floor.

"Get on the move, sailor. We have a life to save."

Rodriguez provided a supply of cloths to absorb the blood, while Fuller spent the next hour removing the shrapnel and suturing the injury with nearly a hundred stitches. Luckily the man had swooned from the pain early on, so there was little screaming. The man woke up with fear in his eyes as Fuller unwrapped his hand to find three fingers severed just at the first knuckle.

"At least it's a clean cut," he remarked to Rodriguez.

"Yes, sir," the orderly replied. "Thank God for that."

"Thank modern warfare," Fuller murmured. "Where's that laudanum? We can afford to give him that small mercy."

"Here, sir." Rodriguez pulled it from a nearby cabinet.

"I need you to talk to him, explain what we're doing. I tried in English, and I need someone to translate." Together they got the man to swallow a draught of the bitter liquid.

"Hold him down, Rodriguez. If he moves, I can't work."

"Yes, sir." He leaned onto the man, who was now moaning with the pain, with Rodriguez holding his wrist with both hands and speaking to him in Spanish in soothing tones. Fuller began rapidly stitching the torn flesh to cover the exposed bone.

"Good job. Last finger, then we've got that head to look at."

"Head?" Rodriguez glanced around.

"A minor scrape, one easy enough for me to handle on my own. Do you need a break, sailor?"

"No, sir."

"Good. See how the man's doing. Ask him how he feels."

Fuller had the fingers stitched by then, and he wrapped them with a bandage as Rodriguez questioned the man. The interchange was as much a one-sided exchange of groans and harshly-grunted invectives, but the orderly finally looked to Fuller and smiled. "He says if you cannot finish faster, just shoot him. It will be more merciful."

"Then he'll live. Tell him we've got to clean and bandage his head. After that, we'll be finished."

As bad as it was, Fuller had to laugh at the man's response to Rodriguez's instructions. He hit his forehead with his good hand and called loudly, "Aieeee!" Then he promptly passed out.

Within little more than an hour, five of the Spanish fleet's ships were burning, sunk, or aground. The final ship found herself unable to run to sea due to the *Oregon* standing a little more than a mile offshore. Fuller felt the *Oregon* shudder as the boom of the ship's 13 inch guns bracketed the fleeing vessel, causing her captain to drive his ship ashore and strike her colors as the ship grounded. The incident stuck in his mind, as the firing of the guns rocked the ship, knocking his shoulder against a corridor wall, and causing a slight bruise. When he made his way topside and asked what had just happened, a sailor pointed out the crippled vessel, explaining what had occurred.

Fuller took note of the sailors' extreme excitement, and having grown to know their moods, he could see this was a momentous event, perhaps even the crux that signaled Spain's upcoming defeat. To keep his record of the events accurate in his mind, just before midnight, he pulled out his journal and paused before beginning his entry. In only a few minutes it would be 4 July, the Independence Day for the United States. Perhaps it would also become a day of celebration for the nation of Cuba. He smiled and began to write:

"A ghostly quiet has come over the ship, and it's good to have the guns silenced. Today we saw the *Cristóbal Colón* attempt her escape, running like a wounded cur, until our own mortars forced her to ground herself. There was more, but I was busy treating Adam Millsap's wound and had no time to notice until the cook's apprentice came with some coffee and sandwiches. He apologized that the mess was closed, and that there would be no dinner served, but I assured him I would have had no time to make it to the mess hall in any case.

"During the confusion surrounding the battle, I was the fool. I failed to duck my head as I made my way down the ship's corridor, and I managed to put a deep gash in my scalp. How I didn't know it was bleeding I can't imagine, but I felt it on my forehead, and I brushed at it, thinking it was water from an overhead pipe, only to have my hand come away red. I had thought Millsap's cut on his leg bad enough, only to have my foolishness eclipse his by a good margin."

Fuller went on to note it was one of the few injuries aboard ship, and it wasn't even caused in support of the war effort. It was carelessness, and he was embarrassed to admit what he'd done. Rodriguez laughed, but Fuller wore his cap most days after that, until he could comb his hair over the injury to disguise the scar.

Two more anxious months passed before the war with Spain drew to a close. During that time, Capt. Clark fell ill, and Capt. A. S. Barker relieved him. During one meal, Fuller overheard the men talking of a man known as "Teddy" Roosevelt. It seemed he had entered Cuba against the Spaniards with a highly-respected group known as the Rough Riders. Fuller reviewed reports of yellow fever and malaria that filtered in from the Army camps on the island itself, although thankfully, there were few such incidents of illness aboard ship. Fuller considered it had to do with cleanliness, something he stressed continually in his duties to the seamen sharing the *Oregon* with him. "Clean quarters are healthy quarters," he preached to them, and the ill things happening to the Army seemed to carry out his mantra. Only 400 men had been killed ashore, and yet 2,000 were affected with disease. It was horrible to consider, but there was nothing Fuller could do in any case.

The *Oregon* sailed for New York on August 14, arriving on August 20. Fuller remained as physician's assistant aboard the *Oregon*, finding quarters in New York as the *Oregon* entered the Brooklyn Navy Yard for overhaul, and leaving out six weeks later to retrace her steps to Rio, the Straits of Magellan, Callao, Peru, and from there to Manila, Philippines, where she was honored to become the flagship for Admiral Dewey under the command of Capt. G. F. Wilde.

Fuller continued with the *Oregon*, traveling to Hong Kong in May of 1900, only to be jarred from his duties when the ship was run aground off the Changshan Islands, flooding her forward hold. At that time, she was put into dry dock at Kure, Japan, and Fuller was released from his shipboard duties and allowed to return to the North American continent for the remainder of his military service. He was sent to Texas, where he celebrated his first night with a buxom redhead, enjoying his time more than all his nights aboard the *Oregon* put together. He awoke the next morning with no regrets and a huge headache. During his time in the military, he kept up with the family and friends through letters and packages.

Winnie Stafford had a daughter named Sally. Janey, his sister, gave birth to another boy, John, who she named for her younger brother. Johnie closed down the saw mill with Joe's consent, since the cost of the timber and construction had slowed until it wasn't profitable on such a small scale. Jake Somerset, the hired hand, left the farm for Alaska, a knapsack on his back and a train ticket in his pocket.

Joe wrote that he and Hannah spent most of their days entertaining the grandchildren. Seldom did he write of the old stage coach days. It was all about the bitumen poured on the forest road, and the settlement of several new neighbors. The space between the old Mozier station and the Sweetwater was rapidly being taken up by cattlemen or farmers. Travelers passed by on their way to resorts and parks built on government land in the mountains. He lamented the loss of the wilderness and grumbled over the sound of civilization creeping ever closer to his domain.

Fuller wrote back of his monotonous life both aboard the *Oregon*—although, he admitted, the battle at Santiago had been charged with tension—and in Texas. It was not as stimulating as San Francisco, but his work was fulfilling, and he began to plan for the future. He was saving his money, he wrote his father; and would soon make a decision. He expected to return to Colorado for a few weeks of recreation after his years in the military but was thwarted by the weather. A heavy storm blew over the mountains and the train schedules were canceled.

He returned to California, a disgruntled and frustrated man. He immediately spent a useless weekend in the gambling saloons and brothels of the Barbary Coast. He rented a room in a cheap hotel and looked around for a new partner.

He'd been in the city less than a month when he awakened one morning, dressed and sat down in the restaurant to eat his breakfast, ham, eggs and biscuits. He took a sip of coffee and picked up his newspaper, as was his custom. He sat up abruptly at the sight of the headlines: SF DOCTOR KILLED IN A LANDSLIDE. It went on to say that Edward Murray, a prominent physician, native of San Francisco, and three miners were killed and fourteen others injured when the area, known as the Klondike, was struck by a minor earthquake. Murray was operating in a temporary hospital near the site of a recent strike, and the snow slide caused massive damage to the hospital. The authorities believed the late spring thaws had caused a log jam on the river. When the quake was felt, the logs descended on the hospital without warning, and all in their path were swept downstream. Murray was not known to have a family, the article said.

Fuller sat stunned at the news, his breakfast unimportant as he thought back to his school days when he first met Edward. They had been introduced by a member of the baseball team, who hoped to swell their ranks by the addition of another player. But, Fuller had no time to spend on sports; his days were filled with anatomy and science studies. He couldn't remember when they'd first talked of becoming partners in San Francisco. Ed had shared about his home in California, and Fuller agreed to visit after his trip in Europe. Somehow, the idea grew through their letters to each other in the next year.

Fuller finished his breakfast, paid his bill and slowly walked to his room, where he read the article again, not believing it could be true that his handsome friend could be dead at such a young age.

*****

In June, Fuller received a letter from his friend Tom Trifold and was pleased to accept a position with a more lucrative practice than when he left. He wrote to his father that he wouldn't be coming home that year after all. He was welcomed to the city by Tom and was soon drawn back into field of medicine.

The new practice was in a separate building from his living quarters and contained not only the multi-partnership firm of Trifold, Hadley and Smith, but on the second floor housed the offices of a dentist and optometrist. The bottom floor had a kitchen and large living area that was shared by all the doctors. The front row of windows faced Montgomery Street and was within walking distance of stores, clothiers and restaurants. He found a small, inexpensive rooming house near downtown and settled down once more to the practice of medicine. With the expert advice of his accountants and banker, he opened an account once more with Hibernia Bank.

He spent one or two days a week at a free clinic for the indigent and actually enjoyed that time more than the society dames of the upper crust and the overweight businessmen of the city. It was an exciting and prosperous time for those with an adventurous and entrepreneurial spirit; the eastern half of the country saw a growing industrialism and societal changes as many families left the farms, and cities grew with the speed of light. Railroad tracks now covered nearly 195,000 miles of ground, and towns grew along the tracks with easier access to produce and manufactured goods. Congress had passed the Gold Standard Act in March of 1900, and Idaho, Wyoming and Utah were admitted into the Union.

The third partner in the practice proved to be older and more experienced than Tom and Fuller, and they often sought him out for advice on puzzling cases. Linus Smith suggested that Fuller put his money into gold, and he took the advice seriously. In the year 1901, James Fuller Hadley's life was changed forever. A few short weeks after the shocking assassination of President William McKinley and the rise to the office of the President of the United States of Theodore Roosevelt in September, Fuller was eating dinner with his crony Tom Trifold and two beautiful females, when they received a message from their housekeeper, Irene Pennell, to come to the hospital at once. They called for hansom cabs for the ladies and met Linus in the doctor's lounge of the surgery department.

Fidel MacDermit had retired, and the hospital was now under the administration of Desmond Manville, a gruff man of wealth and power in the medical field. He had multiple copies of awards and diplomas on his office walls, and interns were known to quake in his presence. But, on this day in late September, Fuller was only interested in the emergency that had called him from a pleasurable evening with his latest mistress. He had used the services of Maude McGowen for several months and rented a small apartment for her near Market Street, where he could visit in the daytime hours without the knowledge of his partners. He wasn't pleased to have his night's plans interrupted.

There had been a boiler explosion on a fishing boat in the harbor, and several of the workers had come to the hospital in critical condition. The force of the blow had damaged the boat moored next to it, and two men and one woman were injured on that vessel. There was chaos at the hospital when he arrived. It would take two surgical rooms and multiple doctors and nurses to treat the victims. Tom was assigned to aid the lady, Linus a wounded fisherman, and Fuller was allocated the owner of the exploded boat. He was deemed to be the most important personage to be treated, and Fuller was amazed to be the surgeon called in for the position. He listened carefully to the details from Dr. Manville and was told that the administrator would be watching from the balcony. Fuller quickly washed his hands and arms, donned the surgical robes of his profession and put soft felt moccasins on his feet. He walked into the operating room, consulted with his team and began to work as he'd been trained and learned through years of experience. He blocked out all other sounds and sights not necessary and worked for four hours, but was pleased with the results. The rest would be taken care of by medications and time.

He walked out of the operating room and, before he could remove his garments, was surrounded by reporters and photographers from the local newspapers. He tried to brush past them, for he was exhausted and hungry, but the crush of people and popping of lights from the cameras encircled him until he made a short, abrupt statement and left them to the authorities. He went to the office shared by his partners and wrote instructions for the nurses, filled in the proper papers required by the hospital and spent the next forty-five minutes writing in detail the facts of the case and what he'd done. He walked to the ward and visited for a few minutes with his indigent patients, wishing them all a good night, voicing instructions for the night nurses and finally, long past dinner time, he was free to go home. He had missed two meals and his stomach was growling in protest. He thought of a short visit with Maude but was too tired.

He unlocked the door, opened his apartment door and almost fell on the bed, still dressed in the clothes of the night before. He was awakened shortly past midnight by the sound of hammering on his door. Groggily, he walked to the door, and there stood Tom in a similar state of exhaustion as Fuller. He came to tell him his patient, Commodore Lionel Fallon, had taken a turn for the worse. Fuller told him to wait and took a quick bath, shaved and put on fresh, clean clothing. He grabbed a couple of pieces of bread and some cheese and ate in the cab on the way to the hospital. Tom told him of the case he'd been called to and the results of the surgery. They compared notes and arrived at the hospital, dark and quiet except for the lights around the entrance doors, and a few lights in the windows.

Tom walked with him up the stairs, entered the patient's room to the chaos of nurses, interns and family members. Tom withdrew, telling him he'd get a cup of coffee from the lounge. Fuller nodded his acceptance and plunged into the melee, his mind now sharp and clear. He ignored the clutter and noise around him and concentrated on his patient's welfare.

An hour later, the commodore was stable and breathing naturally. Fuller sat by his side a few more minutes and walked downstairs to the lounge. There were some stale ham and cheese sandwiches, and the coffee was hot. He filled his belly while he listened to Tom explain the importance of his patient. He was shocked. It seemed the commodore had gained that name as the owner/operator of several fishing boats. His specialty was the salmon of the northern rivers and bays of Oregon. He came to San Francisco once or twice a year for work and pleasure. He owned several salmon canneries in Oregon and Alaska. He had found and invested in gold during the rush that Ed had become a part of before his death in the avalanche. Fuller's name and picture in his doctor's garb, taken after the surgery, was already in the late edition of the leading newspaper in town.

His mind couldn't take it all in, and he asked Tom to find him a bed for the rest of the night, so he could be nearby in case of another setback. He was given a private room on the next floor, and he told the nurse at the desk to call him if he was needed, but surprisingly he wasn't called until nearly noon of the next day. It was Linus who shook his shoulder and awoke him.

"Fuller, wake up. You need to eat and prepare for hospital rounds. We let you sleep as long as we could, but we need help. I'll give you a few minutes to get yourself together and walk you to the doctor's dining room. The hallway is swarming with reporters and photographers, all waiting for you."

"What? Why are they waiting for me? Where's my bag? Is

150

the commodore alright?" He struggled to come out of the fog of sleep. "Damn, my head hurts. What time is it?"

"It's almost noon. We have about an hour to eat and go to the office before our common, ordinary patients start arriving." He looked at Fuller and laughed. "You're a damn hero this morning. The papers say so. I wish I'd been assigned to the commodore instead of a lowly worker type."

"What are you saying? I'm a hero? Surely you're kidding." Fuller took advantage of the facilities and grabbed a cup of coffee. He took a sip and gazed at Linus with amazement.

"It's true. Wait until you read the papers. It's you, alright; Fuller Hadley, blinking at the cameras and wearing your white coat." Linus laughed as they started down the hallway to the private room of the head of the shipping line. As they went, Fuller noticed the stares and whispers they received as they passed. It was so strange, and he needed food badly.

Linus opened the door to the doctor's dining room, and instantly there was silence, then a loud burst of applause. Shouts of congratulations and cheers and good-natured jokes assaulted him; men clapped him on the back; but finally, he was able to get a tray and fill his plate with food. He sat down to eat but was interrupted several times by an intern, or by an older doctor, and he began to believe it was real. But, he hadn't done anything different from what he would have done for the lowest peasant in the tenements. He was embarrassed, and he had trouble swallowing. From across the room, the door opened, and the department head, Desmond Manville, stepped inside. The talking subsided as those who had earlier cheered for Fuller took notice. By the time it was apparent that Manville was headed Fuller's direction, all voices were quiet, and eyes were turned their direction. Manville spoke in a firm voice that Fuller's attendance was required in his office when his rounds were finished, and with an incline of his head, he walked away, nodding to several of the staff, and greeting a female employee on the way out. The encounter was a rock in Fuller's stomach, and his lunch no longer interested him. The clatter of dishes, pots and pans filled the emptiness for a time before the voices started up once again.

Fuller was tempted to visit his famous patient first, but he refrained, went to the wards and dismissed a few who were recovered enough to go home, changed the medication of others, and finally he started in the private rooms, only two of whom were his patients. He told the nurse that Mrs. Frazier could go home, and stepping across the hall, gave a quiet knock and opened the door to the commodore's room. His eyes quickly scanned the room, and he first saw a young woman of average height, dressed in a dark maroon suit of the latest style. Beside her stood an older woman, all in gray. Her gray hair was half-hidden by a large-rimmed gray velvet hat with a large black bow; her dress was of a darker shade, almost purple. The bodice was tight and adorned with small black buttons, and the straight skirt ended just above the tops of shiny black, pointed shoes. She wore spectacles, carried a black handbag and wore black gloves. Fuller moved to the bed and saw his patient, a middle-age man, his face pale and haggard, but his eyes were open, and he lay supine covered with sheets and his hand across his chest. Fuller ignored the ladies and took the man's hand in his; it was soft and his nails neatly trimmed, Fuller had time to notice as he read his pulse.

"Commodore Fallon? I'm Doctor Fuller Hadley, your surgeon. How do you feel? Is there something you need?" He looked around as though searching for something. He found it on the small table in the corner. He had received no answer, and he opened the chart for his patient and glanced at the women. They were gazing at him in shock.

"I thought you were older," came a weak voice from the bed. "I'm glad to be alive; that's how I feel. You look like hell." The man coughed and tried to sit up.

Fuller went to his pillow and helped him raise his head. "You need to keep still, sir. Do want some water?" He turned to the table and poured a small amount from the pitcher into the glass provided. "Just a sip to clear your throat. Does your wound hurt? I can prescribe medicine for that if you need it." He took the glass and placed it on the table. He turned to the ladies and smiled. "Are you related to the commodore? He's going to be fine. It'll take a while for the wound to mend, but he's strong and healthy otherwise."

The older woman stepped forward. "Dr. Hadley, we can't thank you enough. Dr. Manville told us you saved Lionel's life. Your skill and experience, he said, were what turned the trick." She turned to the younger girl, who had been gazing at Fuller with open eyes. "I'm Elizabeth Fallon, and this is our daughter, Eleanor. We were at the Palace Hotel having dinner with friends when we heard the explosion. I never dreamed it was his boat. We didn't know until hours later when one of the crewmen, only slightly wounded, came to us."

Fuller shook her hand and the glove-wrapped hand of the

153

daughter. "How do you do, ma'am, Mrs. Fallon; Miss Fallon."
He turned back to the patient, lying quietly watching the scene.
"You should get some rest, sir. I'll leave something for the pain
at the nurse's desk. I'll be back to visit you this evening. I'm
pleased to meet you all." He walked out of the room without
looking back, and after leaving instructions for the night nurse,
joined Tom and Linus in the doctor's lounge, where they filled
him in on their own day.

The three men worked the rest of the day in their own office
and surgery, and enjoyed a meal of ham steaks, potatoes, carrots
and peas prepared by the housekeeper, Irene. They rode the
cable cars back to the hospital and parted at the door to visit
their individual patients. When Fuller quietly opened the door
of the commodore's room, he was fast asleep. He crept out,
walked through the wet cobblestones to his apartment and spent
a whole night in sleep.

Thirteen

A week after the release of the commodore from the hospital, Fuller received a formal summons to his San Francisco house. It was a magnificent mansion halfway up Sacramento Street. He rode the cable cars to the nearest intersection and presented himself at the door. It was answered by a manservant dressed in a severe dark suit. Fuller presented his card and smiled at the man. The man took his hat and cane and ushered him into the sitting room.

At first glance, it seemed to be filled with tables, a large one in the corner, smaller ones at every chair and sofa, and the surface of the tables filled with lacy doilies and knick-knacks. There was a piano at one wall covered with a huge white scarf, and that was all Fuller had time to notice before the commodore entered the room, walking with a small limp and leaning on a cane.

He was dressed in a black suit, unbuttoned, with a matching vest, white, high starched collar and black string tie. It wasn't too different from what Fuller wore, except his suit was a dark gray.

"Sit down, sir," the commodore commanded, and sat himself in a cushioned seat with wood trim at the top and bottom with curved legs. The cover had a beige background with a floral design and a maroon stripe from top to bottom. The commodore looked pale but healthy, and since Fuller had never seen him outside a hospital bed, he was surprised at how masculine he appeared.

"Thank you, Commodore." And, Fuller sat on the edge of the sofa near the matching chair. He folded his hands in his lap and waited for the man to speak, while his stomach roiled and his pulse raced with nervousness. He'd never been in a situation so fraught with tension, even in his Navy days. After being hounded by newspaper men for the last week, he'd learned to keep a low profile and to try to disguise his appearance.

"Dr. Hadley, would you like some refreshment? I don't indulge in strong drink, but perhaps you might like some brandy?" Fallon gave Fuller a look of inquiry, and Fuller knew a moment of anxiety. If he took the drink, did that mean the man would disapprove of him? He shook his head.

"No, thank you, I'm on my way to the hospital." He smiled. "It wouldn't do to show up before my patients with liquor on my breath."

"Just so. Just so." The commodore nodded his head and sat silently as though observing Fuller's character. "Some tea, perhaps?"

"No, nothing for me, sir." He took a short glance around the room and was struck by a painting on the far wall, opposite the piano. He rose and walked to it. "A Renoir, sir?" He turned and walked back and sat on the sofa. "I admire his work. I saw a few originals when I was in Paris about ten years ago."

"You've been to Paris? France?"

Fuller could see the shipping magnate was excited. He wondered whether he should continue and decided he would. "Yes, I spent a year in Europe: London, Paris, Vienna, Rome. I observed several surgeries while there. It wasn't all pleasure. My father said I was to spend my time wisely. A wise and prudent man, my father." He smiled again. "He ran a relay stage coach station, until the railroads drove such men out of business. Now he's a farmer. I grew up learning to observe the habits of the passengers on the coaches."

"Where was this stage station? I rode the stages when I was younger. But, I prefer to travel by sea." Fallon coughed. "But, you know about that. Tell me about your father's stage station."

"It's in Colorado, among the pine forest with the high mountain peaks in the distance. On the east is a flatter desert climate with scant rain or trees. The old station house is there, but my parents have built a larger house with modern conveniences. A far distance from the sea, you would find it."

"Ah, I've never been that far inland. Well. Well. I asked you to come see me to offer you a reward for saving my life, but I've begun to change my mind. With that background, I can see that a sum of money might be objectionable. Maybe some other way to show my appreciation would be appropriate?"

Fuller could see the man was testing him, and he straightened his shoulders. "No. If you feel an obligation, perhaps you might donate some token to the hospital or to the medical college. I need nothing for myself. It's my profession. The satisfaction of seeing you healthy is all I desire."

"Ah, a modest young man. I read something about you in the newspapers. You have two partners. Perhaps they might gain by a reward?"

"As for that, I can't say, sir. I really must be going. Hospital duty calls me." Fuller rose and prepared to leave, thinking the visit was over.

"Wait. Ring that bell by the door, will you please? I had meant to introduce you to my wife and daughter."

Fuller walked to the heavy velvet pull rope with the gold tassel and yanked on it. The manservant appeared as though he had been standing near the door. He bowed, "Yes, sir?"

"James, tell my wife that I request her presence in the drawing room, and Eleanor, too, if you please." The servant bowed and left the room. Fuller sat back down and discreetly drew his timepiece from his pocket and looked at the face. He looked up in time to see a frown on the commodore's face, but he didn't care; his time was precious to him.

The two women he had met in the hospital strolled into the room, and Fuller was able to observe them more closely, without the pressure of his duties as a physician. The wife was wearing a dark, full length dress in a wine color, with high stiff collar and tight wrist bands. It had an ornament of some sort at the neck. As he bowed over her hand, he observed it was a peacock with its jeweled tail spread wide, and he thought it to be made of gold filigree.

The daughter was dressed in a two-piece suit, of a shade of blue that complimented her eyes, which were gray or blue; the top had a white collar and cuffs with a black belt, and she also had a pin on her bodice. It looked to be a timepiece from the design. Her hair was a shade of reddish-brown that was quite attractive and piled high on her head in a loose pompadour, much like his sister Janey wore the last time he saw her.

"Pleased to meet you, Miss Fallon. I trust you are well." Fuller didn't realize that he'd made a joke until the girl burst out laughing. He gave her an inquisitive glance.

"My goodness, Doctor. Are you trying to gain more business? I assure you I am quite well, and my mother, also." She looked at her father, as if for guidance.

"I beg your pardon. I was being polite. I meant no offense." Fuller followed her eyes and saw a frown on the shipping magnate's face. There seemed to be an undercurrent in the room he didn't understand.

"Of course not. Elly, you're too quick to see the unusual and humorous. Dr. Hadley, I'm grateful for your care of my husband. Would you be kind enough to have dinner with us this evening? It won't be anything fancy, just family and a few friends. Eight of the clock?" Liz Fallon was gracious, and Fuller was intrigued at the reason for her invitation. He'd like to know more, so he accepted.

"Yes, thank you. I believe I would enjoy it. But, truly, I must leave you. I have patients waiting at the hospital." He walked toward the door and was surprised to see the manservant was there to show him out. He turned back and saw a gleam of mischief in the eyes of Eleanor Fallon and looked sharply at her father, who was attempting to rise, using the cane to good effect.

"Please, sir. Don't put stress on your wounds. I'll see you tonight, then?" He saw him nod, and he left the room and the house after accepting his hat and cane from the servant. He heard the click of the door as he walked down the steps. His mind was racing with speculation as he strode toward the intersection where he caught the cable car and rode to the hospital. Something was afoot, and he was curious to know what it might be.

*****

Fuller arrived at the Fallon mansion door that evening at ten minutes of the hour. He hesitated to call early, but assumed they understood the schedule of the public transportation. He greeted the manservant by name.

"Good evening, James. The weather seems to be continued mild, and I suspect a fog will roll in before morning. What do you think?" He handed James his hat and lightweight overcoat. Although it was late summer, the nights grew cold on the coast. He smiled at the man's reply.

"Yes, sir. A fog is sure to come in before dawn. The family is waiting in the drawing room, sir." The man's eyes shone with a gleam that Fuller couldn't interrupt. He decided to ignore it.

Indeed, the parlor seemed to be filled with people. He hadn't expected that. And, before he could grasp the significance, he was introduced to first one lady and her husband, and then another, until he was standing in front of Miss Eleanor Fallon, dressed in a white frock of lace and silk, perhaps. Fuller wasn't conversant in the materials used in a female's dress; he only knew what he liked, and this dress was very becoming. It had free-flowing sleeves to the elbow that draped over the shoulder and to the beaded bodice. The floor-length skirt was tight through the waist and hips, and widened at the knees with stitchery that reminded Fuller of his grandmother's embroidery, and the train swept majestically behind her as she walked gracefully across the room. Her soft, reddish-brown hair was piled high above her head, and he could just see the whisper of sparkling jewels in the strands. His heart began to race at an alarming clip.

"Good evening, Dr. Hadley." She said, as she lowered her eyes modestly. She held out a dainty hand covered in thin, lacy white gloves.

"Miss Fallon." He bowed and was able see a small, beaded white bag at her waist, hanging from a silver chain. He smiled and turned to her mother. "Mrs. Fallon."

Everyone stood around in small groups, and Fuller was fascinated by the colorful gowns, the facial hair on the men and the amount of liquor they seemed able to consume. He had attended social dinners before, but not on this grand scale, and he seemed to be the main attraction, by the sly glances and whispers behind the ladies' fans. He took it all in with a word of gratitude when a compliment was intended, and with a modest bow when called for. He was relieved when the servant announced that dinner was served.

He was seated next to Eleanor on his right and a matronly woman in deep purple on his left. The crystal chandelier hung high above the table and sparkled with the multi-colored glow of candles. In the center of the long table was a fragrant display of blooming flowers and candle holders with flickering tapers placed here and there to shed a gleam onto the silver and crystal glassware. The dishes were stark white and held a thin gold rim.

"Dr. Hadley, I've heard so much about you. Do you take private patients?" asked Mrs. Millicent Gardner, the lady in the purple dress.

"Yes, I'm a member of the medical partnership, Trifold, Hadley and Smith. We're located near St. Michael's Hospital on Cedar Hill Lane. But, I don't discuss my practice during my leisure hours, if you would excuse me, Mrs. Gardner." She turned from him with an angry snort, and Fuller supposed that would be the end of the conversation on his left. But, she continued to turn to him occasionally with frivolous obser-vations and gossip about the other guests, and he was forced to reply.

On the other side, Eleanor preened and ate with gusto for a well-brought-up, polite female, and Fuller was able to learn more about her than she perhaps realized. She had a governess when a child, had attended a boarding school in Philadelphia, ridden on her father's fishing boats, and loved to feel the wind and spray on her face. She had a friend named Inez Conant. She discreetly pointed her out, sitting near the end of the table, between a young gentleman looking ill-at-ease in a dark suit and high collar, and an older gentleman who was her father, Benjamin Conant.

The dinner seemed to never end, but at last the women withdrew to the parlor, and the men sat and discussed politics, the banking industry, which Fuller realized a couple were engaged in, and the heightened industrialization of the eastern

United States, and how it would affect the economy. When Mr. Conant and the commodore began to discuss corruption along the Barbary Coast, Fuller's ears pricked up, for he had friends there, and patients who desired to remain anonymous. His friend Tom Trifold was a frequent visitor to the brothels and dancing halls.

Commodore Fallon's face became red and his eyes gleamed with an unholy light when he talked of the corruption and graft of the city. Fuller was hard pressed not to laugh. He doubted if the gentleman had ever stepped foot in the establishments. It was an entertaining and enlightening hour, but Fuller soon made his excuses and asked James to call him a cab. He graciously thanked his host and hostess and went on his way. Just as he had predicted, a fog covered the city as he made his way to his apartment and paid off the cabby.

Fourteen

Fuller thought that would be the end of his association with the Fallon family; but within the next few months he became more entwined with the social class in which they dwelt. His introduction to Mrs. Gardner and Benjamin Conant soon had him dining and attending the theater and the opera with his new set of friends, until his partner, Linus Smith, cautioned him against too close a fraternization with the wealthy and frivolous society of the city.

He found himself more than a few times partnered with Eleanor Fallon, and he enjoyed her company. When the subject of marriage was first mentioned, he shrugged it aside. He continued to visit his mistress regularly and had no plans for marriage. He seemed to find pleasure in two directions: that of a sober, hard-working doctor, working in the slums and tenements of the city, and the cosmopolitan man of the town, wined and dined in the best homes and restaurants by the wealthy and leisurely class. It was bound to come to a head, and on a perfect warm night in April, it did.

Fuller was feeling tired and out of sorts after receiving a letter from his father inviting him to spend the month in Colorado where the trees were tall and fragrant, the roses in Vanessa's yard beginning to bloom and the children growing beyond recognition. He began to long for the sight of the mountains and mentioned it to the commodore's wife at a dinner party held for the celebration of the marriage of Miss Inez Conant and Mr. Ezra Kendall, whom he had met at that first dinner party in September. Without thinking, he drank two glasses of wine with the meal, knowing that he wasn't scheduled for work that night.

A toast was made to the couple, and Fuller drank a glass of champagne with everyone else, and the waiter brought another. He began to feel dizzy and went into the library to spend a quiet moment alone before making his departure. He remembered asking James to call him a cab, and he used the water closet, but nothing after that. He awoke the next morning in the bed of Miss Eleanor Fallon, his arms around her pale body. He sat up in shock.

"What? How the hell did I get here?" He looked at the woman, and she gave a lazy, seductive smile and bared her breasts to him. He jumped from the bed and looked for his trousers, but it was too late.

The commodore and Mrs. Fallon burst into the room, and she began to yell about her poor daughter being seduced by him. Commodore Fallon threatened to have him horsewhipped or worse if he didn't make restitution immediately for his transgression. Fuller stood stark naked in the boudoir of an innocent woman and quickly grabbed for the first article he could find to cover himself. The commodore strode to the bed, Eleanor moved aside and there Fuller could see a bright red stain, clear evidence of his guilt. Fuller realized in a moment that he had been most thoroughly trapped and had no choice but to accept the inevitable. He saw the gleam of satisfaction in Eleanor's eyes and the handkerchief that Mrs. Fallon wielded with a sly glance, and Fuller began to pull on his pants.

The wedding was announced in the newspaper a day later, and the lawyers were called in. The hospital officials seemed pleased, his partners were shocked but his mistress was the most upset of all. When she saw the file picture of him taken after the wreckage of the boat; she summoned Fuller to her side.

The argument was soon over. Fuller stood, humble and subdued, as the woman shrieked at him and threw her brush at his head. Unfortunately, he didn't duck fast enough and received a small bruise on the forehead, while he found himself tongue-tied to explain about his future bride and his friends. He cancelled the lease on the apartment, and she threatened to sue, but backed away when she found an older, wealthier lover.

He asked Tom Trifold to be his best man and visited the clothier to buy a tuxedo, which he couldn't afford, so borrowed the sum from Linus. He visited the courthouse to obtain the license. He tried to smile and looked pleased, but his heart and mind weren't in the preparations, nor in the engagement party and dance thrown by the bride's family. He lost weight, his face became haggard and his eyes were dull with his attempts to keep up his heavy schedule at the hospital, the work in the clinic for the indigent and the frivolous entertainments of his society friends. The only good to come from the event was that his bank account increased by a tremendous amount with the bride's dowry. He spent the last night of his bachelorhood writing a long letter to his father and on his knees in prayer that all would go well in the future.

The first day of May dawned bright and sunny, with the scent of spring flowers in the air, as Fuller and Tom in their tuxedoes and Linus in his best suit rode to the church. Tom kept fingering the ring in his pocket, and Linus stared out the window with a gloomy face. Fuller tried to cheer his friends, but his stomach was roiling, and his head ached. They had the cabby stop at the post office so he could mail his letter, and as he dropped it into the slot, he thought, surprisingly, of Standing Tree and the beaded bag that hung on his parents' dining room wall. It was as though the old man was wishing him a happy life. It was a foolish thought, but Fuller couldn't seem to shake it as he stood before the huge crowd and said his wedding vows with a strong determined voice. Eleanor stood in pale blue, her face and hair covered with a heavy veil, and he couldn't see her eyes. She responded with a weak, shy voice, and it was done.

They walked out of the church and rode in a surrey decorated with white ribbons. Behind them trailed a noisy passel of old shoes and tin cans. They moved slowly over the cobblestones to the Palace Hotel, where the reception was to be held. They stood behind a large cake and shook hands with the guests until Fuller thought he would faint from the heat and the smell of perfume. He smiled and bowed to the mayor, the prestigious Mr. Levi Ellert and his wife. Beside him, Eleanor seemed quiet and pale. She gave the mayor a weak smile and kept her eyes on the floor. Finally, it was over, and they retired to the suite reserved for them by the bride's father.

The nightmare was not finished with the wedding. When Fuller climbed into the bed beside his bride, she began to cry. He tried to comfort her using a soft, gentle tone. She cringed from him as though in fear, leapt from the bed and ran into the water closet and locked the door.

He rose and draped himself in his robe. He whispered at the door, "Eleanor, what's wrong, darling? It's alright. We're married now. Anything that happened before is all forgotten. Eleanor?" He waited a few minutes, but all he heard was weeping.

He raised his voice. "Eleanor, please come out. I don't understand. You seemed to welcome my advances on the night of the party, although I don't really remember anything after I drank the champagne." He stood looking across the room and out the window. He could see nothing but a reflection of himself in the glass. The heavy drapes hung to the floor limp and longer than needed. He crossed the room and pulled the drapes closed. He heard the click of the door, and his bride walked out, her eyes cast firmly on the floor.

"Eleanor, what's happened? Tell me, darling, and I'll make it right. Do you need some time to get used to me? Come, sit down, and we'll talk."

But, she raised the covers and slid under them, and Fuller saw that as a signal that she had finished her reluctance. He joined her in the bed, but lay on his back and stared at the ceiling. He noticed a water stain in the plaster.

He spoke quietly, "Dear, talk to me. What have I done? Do

you need more time? I don't understand. On the night of the party, you were willing." He scratched his head. "At least I think you were; I can't remember. You let your parents think I'd seduced you. Why are you shy of me now? Was it something I did or said at the wedding?" She remained silent, stiff and tightly wrapped in the blankets.

He tried once more. "Eleanor, sit up and tell me what's wrong. How have I offended you?" He shook her gently on the shoulder; she cringed away, mumbling something under her breath.

Finally, with a total disregard for her modesty, he mounted her and plunged, only to find that his bride was a virgin. He leapt from the bed, his skin crawling with confusion. The cool air on his damp skin wasn't enough; his hands tightened into fists, and she drew back and covered herself. Her eyes seemed enormous. He reached for his robe and stood as still as one of the marble statues he had seen in Europe on his Grand Tour.

"Why? What had I done that you and your parents would treat me so?" He ran his hand through his hair. He saw a chair beside the door, fell into it and put his head in his hands, his shoulders quaking with anger and dismay. Long, jagged whimpers of pain and disgust overwhelmed him, until he felt he would collapse from it. His heart thumped, and his knees quivered. Finally, he lifted his head and asked again, "Why?"

As though from a deep well of resentment, the explanation came in bursts of temper and tears. "Mother planned it. She said I'd never find a better husband. She planned it all from the first night. She said you'd be kind, loyal and generous. I begged her to let me marry Frederic Morse, but she wouldn't hear of it. I've

169

loved Fred since we were children. But, he's poor; he works on the boat, the one that exploded. He was injured badly but survived. Oh, I'm sorry, I knew it was wrong, but Mother said after the wedding you'd be amenable and accept the situation." Her eyes seemed to glow with guilt, and while Fuller couldn't help but be compassionate, he wanted the facts.

"What happened that night? How did I get in your bed? And, the blood on the sheet?" He frowned and gazed at the white bedclothes tumbled around her now. With a determined step, he walked to the bed and grabbed the covers from her and looked down. Yes, there it was: finally, evidence of her virginity, unmistakable and permanent. He threw the sheets back over the woman, and she wrapped them around her.

She raised a finger. "I cut my finger so it would bleed, not too much, Mother said, just enough to prove your seduction so that Father would force the marriage."

"He thought it was real? That I had seduced you?"

"Yes, she said that would happen. She said that all we had to do was get you into my bed; you'd be so drunk you'd not know what happened."

"Who brought me upstairs, James?"

"Yes, he gave you some laudanum in the champagne and you passed out on the sofa. He and one of the waiters helped you upstairs, and then when the guests had gone, I went up and undressed and waited for you to wake up. I was to act pleased and sated." Her eyes began to fill with tears again.

"You're a good actress, I'll give you that. I was totally convinced, although I couldn't remember a thing. And, tonight? What was all that about? Were you frightened that I wouldn't complete the charade? That I'd leave you alone and sleep on the floor? What were your plans after the wedding?" He glared at her and she cowered in the bed.

"I didn't think about that. I didn't think about it at all. We weren't supposed to get married. Fred said he'd help me get away, then we could embark on one of the fishing boats and he'd take care of me. Please, forgive me, and release me from the marriage."

"Fred? You mean Frederic Morse who works on your father's boat?"

"He's my lover." She threw her words at him in defiance. "He loves me."

For the first time, Fuller began to see or thought he saw that she was sincere, but it was too late.

"What about your reputation? And, mine? My God, I'm a doctor. Do you think anyone would trust me with their family if I sought an annulment? You didn't think about that, did you?" He rose and strode about the room, agitated and angry. "No, we have to put it behind us and go on with the marriage. I'm sorry for your friend, but we can't change the facts. You gave your word to God and the people who heard you tonight. I'm tired. Go to sleep. We'll plan what to do in the morning." He pointed his finger at her, a fierce anger in his gaze. "But, I won't tolerate any meetings behind my back with that man, Fred. That's over, do you hear? I won't have people whispering about my wife's lover."

He went into the water closet and washed himself, and when he came back out, searched for the extra blanket usually kept in hotel rooms, grabbed a pillow from the bed and made a pallet on the floor. As he turned his back, clothed only in his robe, he could hear her crying long into the night, but he had no sympathy for her.

The next morning, he waited for her to awaken and dress, and they went down to breakfast. Neither ate much; she nibbled on toast and drank a cup of tea. He ate eggs, biscuits and ham, and they tasted like the dust on his father's saw mill floor. He had taken three weeks for a wedding trip and still planned the trip to Colorado to introduce her to his parents, but first a trip to the commodore's home was required.

Dr. Fuller Hadley stood on a warm spring day outside his in-laws' house, his determination strong and his resolve clear to the woman standing beside him, fashionably dressed in a dark, forest green dress with a large brimmed hat with an even larger white bow on top; there was a thin green veil to match her dress, and she looked lovely in the sunshine.

The door was answered by James. He stepped back in fear, his eyes wide in horror. "Yes, sir?"

"Tell the commodore I wish to see him, immediately." He gave no quarter, but pushed Eleanor in front of him, and she meekly made her way into the parlor.

James retreated to the far side of the entrance hall and stumbled through a doorway, furtively glancing at Fuller as he disappeared inside. Fuller snorted in disgust, and he followed Eleanor into the parlor. He paused and looked at the furnishings with new eyes. The first time he'd visited he'd been impressed and awed by its splendor, but with the events of the preceding weeks, it had become a mere mockery of what he'd hoped his life to become. He dismissed the whole scene at a glance, no longer caring for the carved finials and the elegant fabrics. He turned to the door when the commodore came in.

"Fuller? Eleanor? What's toward? I thought you'd be at the ferry terminal this morning." The elder man's eyes were puzzled, and Fuller began to wonder how much he knew.

He pressed Eleanor to the front. He knew her eyes were red-rimmed and her face pale, in spite of the rouge with which she tried to hide the results of her weeping.

"Speak, Eleanor." Fuller watched the shipping magnate's face as Eleanor complied, her tears beginning anew.

"I'm sorry, Father." She ran to a chair and sat down, her head in her hands, sobbing. "Nothing's going the way I planned."

"Nothing? What do you mean? Surely not your marriage. I thought you loved Dr. Hadley." Mr. Fallon moved slowly and painfully to her side.

"Oh, Father. Never. How could you believe that? Mother said it would all work out; now we have to stay married and go to Colorado. Oh, Papa, how could you treat me this way, your only child? I'm so confused and unhappy."

The commodore looked as shocked as Fuller had felt last night. "What? What do you mean, daughter? Are you in love with someone else?"

Eleanor looked up, her eyes red and her face streaked with her tears. "How can you not know my feelings? It's always been Fred. You've refused to see it."

"Fred? Do you mean Fred Morse, my fishing boat attendant? Fuller, please explain what's happened." The commodore leaned on his cane and seemed about to collapse.

"Come, sir, and sit down. Do you need something? Some water?" Automatically, as naturally as breathing, the doctor in Fuller overtook his anger and disgust.

"No. No. I'm fine." The man leaned on his cane. His color began to come back, and he gazed at his daughter, who was sniffling into her lace-bound handkerchief. His eyes revealed the shock at his daughter's words, and Fuller began to reassess the man's complicity in the matter. Fuller sat on the sofa, as far from Eleanor, but as close to his father-in-law as possible, in case he was needed. He regretted that he'd left his medical bag in the hotel room.

"Sir," Fuller began, "I was deceived by you, your daughter and your wife. I accepted my guilt in the matter that took place some weeks ago, although I had no remembrance of it. The evidence seemed to prove my actions, but now I know I wasn't guilty, and I will not continue to be accused of something I had no part in. What your daughter is trying to say, sir, is that I took my rightful place last night as her husband and found to my dismay that she was a virgin, still."

"Daughter!" The commodore's voice shook with disbelief. "You led us to believe this man misused you."

Eleanor dropped her head and burst into tears once more, leaving Fuller to take up his own defense once again.

"Sir, it was all a deception, of which I believe you must have also taken part. I was drugged at the party by your manservant, James, and with the help of one of the waiters, led upstairs and undressed to await your daughter."

"Impossible!" The commodore sputtered.

"I have it in your daughter's own words. I awoke as you

174

found me. The guilt was not mine. Ask your daughter, sir, and your wife." He saw the continued emotions on Fallon's face and accepted that although the man may have wished for the marriage, he'd also been deceived by the manner of its coming into fruition.

"Daughter, is this true, what Fuller claims? He didn't seduce you? He's innocent in this matter?"

"Oh, Father, everything has gone so wrong. Mother made me do it; she said Fuller wouldn't know. She said he was such a womanizer, he wouldn't discover the deception, and I would have a happy life. She said he'd take the dowry and be grateful, and I would have a respectful place in society, but now I know Fuller won't be satisfied with me." Her tears had begun to fade, and she pouted and twisted the handkerchief. "He says we're married, and I can't have Fred."

"Of course not, child. You're a married woman, now. How could you expect any different?" Her father pulled a cloth from a pocket and patted sweat from his forehead.

"Fred said he'd come for me before the ceremony, and we'd go away on one of your boats. I didn't intend to marry Fuller at all." She burst into hot, wracking tears, and Fuller began to wonder how a woman could cry so much.

Suddenly, the room seemed filled with people. First, Fred Morse entered, rumpled and distraught, as if he'd been in a panic the night through. He lurched toward Fuller, as if to demand something, but Fuller shrugged and motioned toward the wailing Eleanor. Mr. Fallon made his way to a chair as Fred went to Eleanor and put his arms around her. She fell into them with relief, and Fuller knew that while her boast of them as

175

lovers might not be true, she hadn't lied to him about their love, at least.

The commodore called out very loudly, "Can anyone in this household give me an explanation?"

James rushed in. "Sir, I can explain."

He was drowned out by Mrs. Fallon, following behind him. Fuller stood as his mother-in-law strode fiercely into the room. Her eyes flashed with anger as she pushed James out of her way, and the manservant retreated to the back of the room. She glanced around, saw Fred with his arms around Eleanor and walked to Fuller. She stood inches from him and thrust her finger in front of his face.

"My daughter is in tears. This should be the happiest day of her life. What do you mean, treating my precious Eleanor this way? We'll be the talk of society. We'll be disgraced."

"Dear," Mr. Fallon called to her.

"Lionel," she interrupted, swinging one arm and pointing to her daughter. "You must do something. This cannot be allowed to happen." She turned back to Fuller and slapped him across the face. "It's your fault. Why didn't you take her to Colorado like you planned?"

Fuller stood perfectly still, his face burning from her palm and his anger mounting, but he didn't speak. It was a struggle to keep his hands from her. He saw Fred Morse lead Eleanor from the room, but at the moment, his only focus was on the harsh things he wished to say to Mrs. Fallon.

"Liz, sit down and be quiet until I get to the heart of this drama. Fuller, please sit down. I need a drink." Fallon rapped his cane heavily on a tabletop, and he coughed. "James, where's my drink?"

James went to the drinks cabinet, poured a small amount of brandy into a glass and handed it to Lionel Fallon, who downed it in one quick swallow and placed the glass on the table beside his chair.

"Speak!" he roared, and James began to explain.

"It's like this, sir. Mrs. Fallon told me that Miss Fallon couldn't marry Mr. Morse because he's of the worker class, not good enough for her. When you were injured in the explosion, she saw Dr. Hadley and decided he would be a good, loyal husband, him being a doctor as he is. Then, you seemed to want the match, and Miss Fallon and Dr. Hadley seemed to enjoy each other's company, so I thought you approved of the things I done."

"What did you do, James?" The commodore's tone was softer, as if he wasn't sure he wanted to hear the answer.

"The night of the party, I went to Mrs. Fallon's room, and she gave me a little laudanum in a bottle. I poured it in Dr. Hadley's glass. That's when Mr. Conant made the toast to his daughter and her intended, and I kept an eye on Dr. Hadley. I knew how laudanum worked because my mother took it for her terrible headaches." He seemed to be hesitant about saying more, and Fuller wondered who had prescribed it.

"Well, go on. What happened then?" Fallon impatiently inquired.

"I gave a dollar to the waiter hired for the night, and we carried Dr. Hadley upstairs and undressed him, and left the room. I don't know what happened after that, sir. I went on with my duties until the next morning. I believe Mrs. Fallon told you that the doctor was in Miss Fallon's room, but as to that, I can't say." James looked deflated, like a punctured hot air dirigible.

The silence in the room could have been cut with a cleaver. Fuller sat, stunned and sick. Mrs. Fallon sniffed and looked at her husband. Mr. Fallon gazed at the floor as though in a daze.

The commodore looked up at last, only then seeing that his daughter's chair was vacant. "James, where is my daughter?"

Everyone looked around, and Fuller remembered the couple making their escape. He realized she and Fred were gone. Not gone from the room, but from the house. His sickness overcame him, and with a hand over his mouth, he ran to the water closet and lost the contents of his stomach. The heaves wracked his body until there was nothing left to do but wipe his face and hands and return to the parlor, where he found an uneasy silence. James was gone. Mrs. Fallon was sitting near the window, gazing out with her eyes puffy and red. The commodore was sitting at a desk, writing something on a sheet of paper.

"Ah, Fuller, you're back." He turned from the desk. "I've written a note to my friend the mayor, and one to Judge Harper. We'll have the marriage quietly annulled as quickly as possible. I can't say how much I regret this contretemps. It's obvious that my daughter doesn't want to remain in the marriage. I've sent a note to the captain of the *Sarah Ann*. If it is as I suspect, Fred and Eleanor are on the boat and will remain unless we have them arrested and dragged off. It's scheduled to depart for Alaska this afternoon. If I had known of the wicked scheme, I'd never have let you be dishonored in this way. Please, accept my apologies."

"What about my reputation, sir? Can you restore that? Can

you correct the damage that's been done to the patients who trusted me with their lives?" He laughed bitterly. "A few months ago, Commodore Fallon, I didn't know you and your daughter existed. I was called from a party to the hospital to attend to you. Can you restore the weeks this forced engagement has stolen from me? And what of the reputation that I enjoyed at that time?"

"Man, don't be a fool. My wife has told me of her complicity in this matter. I had no wish to entrap an innocent man. You cannot blame me."

"No? I feel differently, sir. I'll go to the bank and see the dowry is returned to you. Do what you will about the annulment. I intend to catch the train as planned and go home to my family, where honor and duty are still held in esteem. Good day, sir. Mrs. Fallon, goodbye."

He went directly from the bank to his office, and in a few short, solemn sentences told Tom and Linus what had happened and asked them to bear the publicity as best they could. He was torn between relief and sorrow as he picked up his luggage and his bulging medical bag, and took a cab to the ferry station, cancelled his wife's ticket and waited silently in a corner for the departure of the ferry to be announced.

Fifteen

More than twenty-five hours later the train chugged into the Denver station and stopped with a groan and a puff of steam as though it were as tired as its passengers. For the last hour, Fuller had been trying in his head to think of words to tell his parents and sister and brother how his marriage had ended before it had begun. He'd decided halfway through the trip that he was a coward, that he should have fought for the marriage, not meekly acquiesced to an annulment. The further he rode, the angrier he became until he saw the mountains from a window as the train rounded a curve. There in the beauty of the day and the wondrous sight that met his eyes, he realized the decision had been the right one. Why should he try to hold on to a reluctant bride? With a wisdom gained from experience and inheritance, Fuller Hadley knew that Eleanor would have left him at some future date, and it was better for her to go now than later.

He lifted his medical bag, his coat and a small personal bag he had carried onto the train, and he walked the aisle and down the steps. He took a deep breath and looked for a familiar face. Johnie stepped forward with his wife, Vanessa. The children weren't there, and Fuller knew the surrey wouldn't have held them all. Vanessa searched in vain for Eleanor, and a puzzled look crossed her face.

"Where's the bride? Did you leave her behind?" Johnie asked, his eyes alive with mischief.

"Yes. I did. I'll explain when we get home. Please, don't ask questions now. Here's my ticket stub for the luggage. Vanessa, how have you been? Are the roses in bloom? I've looked forward for days to seeing your garden. The children, are they well?" Fuller smiled and kept his head high and his shoulders straight as he fielded the curious glances and inquisitive looks. He shook hands with Tater and asked him to wait for the answers, too. They lifted his luggage onto the flat-bed wagon and tied it securely with the ropes. Tater gave him a sympathetic smile and mounted the wagon. Johnie lifted the whip and touched the back of the horse, and the wheels began to roll.

The vehicles came out of the gloom of the forest, and Fuller filled his lungs and his nostrils with the smells so familiar to him. His gaze rose to the mountains and saw they were covered with clouds. He broke the silence.

"Looks like rain tonight. What do you think, Johnie? You're more familiar with the weather than I am." His brother had no time to answer, for as soon as the surrey and wagon were sighted, they were flanked with children, both tall and short. A scattering of chickens flew into the air, clucking in protest. Three dogs began barking, and out of sheer release of tension,

Fuller began to laugh. He leapt from the surrey and tried all at once to gather the children into his arms, as they shouted and tried to be the first to gain his attention. They didn't notice there was no bride sitting beside him.

Fuller looked up and saw standing on the porch a man and a woman, his arm on her shoulder, and as though a dam broke, he untangled himself from the clambering children and dogs, leaped the steps and threw himself into his mother's arms. She patted his back and cried hot, healing tears. She released him and stepped back. Joe grabbed him in a bear hug

"Welcome home, son."

"Yes, Papa, I'm home." And, San Francisco and all his troubles were far behind. He wiped his eyes, and he gave one quick glance to the far distant mountains and entered the house, his arms around his folks. "How have you been, Papa? Have you any new horses? Mama, I could sure use a slice of your apple pie. I'm as hungry as a mule after crossing the sand dunes. Do you think I could have a bath? The soot and dust of the road have coated my hair and skin like a blanket." He tried not to be angry when Joe looked at the surrey. There would be plenty of time for explanations later. He had almost a month free of responsibilities, and he planned to fill every moment with pleasant memories for the bad times ahead when he'd have to face his other life once more.

Sixteen

When the rain came, it passed with a fury that Fuller remembered all too well. The hail and rain fell on the roof, and the wind whistled around the house. The shutters clattered against the frames, and the fire in the fireplace shot up sparks from the logs. The dogs began to howl and moan. Fuller heard the sound of a falling tree, and he looked at his family.

Walter shrugged his shoulders, Janey hugged her husband, and Winnie Stafford held her latest, a son named Jasper, close in her arms. Beside her, Tater said, "Some more firewood to cut, Joe." And, Joe raised his coffee cup and smiled. He'd seen it many times before. Fuller knew they had been patient, and now with most of the children asleep on pallets or in the bedrooms, he decided it was time to confess.

"Papa, Mama, I know you've been waiting to know what happened, and I don't want to dramatize it more than necessary, but you've been patient, and I thank you for that. It was all a hoax, a deception." His eyes went to his coffee cup, and he took a sip, not surprised at the gasps of dismay.

"It started, I think, with Commodore Fallon. As I wrote, I was called out one night when a fishing boat exploded in the harbor. I worked for several hours, sewing up wounds, using my skill as I'd been taught and experienced many times before. You wrote that you read about it in the papers. I was as astonished as anyone when I was told who he is and how influential and wealthy. I became a part of the society, and I guess I let it bother me more than I realized." He looked around at the crowd of people in the room: Joe and Hannah, Janey and Walter, Johnie and Vanessa, Tater and Winnie and the new hired hand, Woody Hakon, whom he had just met that day. He took another sip of coffee, thus emptying the cup, and set it on the table at his elbow.

"I relished the parties, the dances, the dinners, and felt it was my due; my reward. I never thought it would come to the end that it did. I attended the engagement party of a couple of friends; just one of the crowd. The names wouldn't mean anything to you. I drank a couple of glasses of wine at dinner; I wasn't expected at the hospital that night, or I'd never have touched it. I drank a toast to the bride and groom, as everyone else did. They all knew that. It's not an excuse, but an explanation of why the drug hit me so hard." Another gasp was heard, and he paused, his mind in turmoil.

"I felt dizzy after that glass of champagne and thought I'd withdraw until I felt better. That was all I remembered until the next morning, when I found myself naked in Eleanor's bed. She was in on the deception, although I know now, she was as deceived as I."

He appealed to Joe, "What could I do, Papa? I looked guilty. I felt guilty. Her mother and father burst in the room, and I was trapped. The only honorable thing was to marry the girl. So, the commodore and his lady planned this big wedding, and all the influential people including the mayor were invited. I wrote you that I planned to bring Eleanor here for our wedding trip. I received the month off, since I hadn't had a holiday in years. The notoriety over saving the shipping magnate's life helped, I suppose. The rest is rather anti-climax. We made our vows, signed our names and celebrated with everyone. It was when we were alone in the hotel room that she couldn't keep it a secret any longer."

"What happened?" That was Janey, always the eager one.

"What do you think happened, darling sister? She pretended to be a shy, innocent bride; I pressed her, thinking I had seduced her, so she couldn't be innocent." He couldn't sit; he had to rise and move around the room. "But, she was, Papa." He looked at Joe as though he was the only one who would understand. He continued to speak only to his father. "I was harsh and cruel, looking back, but I believed the lies. I thought she wanted what I could give. I thought she was ready, and just trying to be brave. She was a virgin." It was said with a clear, bold statement. And the silence was as loud as the thunder rolling across the sky outside the walls. "She was innocent of that at least." He paused again and looked at the other listeners.

"I was shocked, of course, devastated. I had, in my ignorance, done what I'd been publicly accused of. I demanded an explanation. My precious, innocent bride had a lover, although they hadn't consummated their whispered vows to

185

each other. I guess she was waiting for a miracle. I know Fred was."

"Fred?" It was only a name, but all eyes were glued to Fuller's face for the answer.

"Yes, Johnie. Fred. It seems they've loved each other for years. He worked on the fishing boat and was injured on the night of the explosion. My friend Linus tended him, but his injuries weren't serious. Her mother wouldn't think of a marriage between them. He was lower class, not worthy. I was a doctor, fully trained. I'd been to the cities of Europe, came from a respectable family, though not in society standards, and I had saved the commodore's life. I was chosen as the victim. Mrs. Fallon knew that I wouldn't have married Eleanor, if left on my own. She started with cunning and subtlety. I thought about it a lot on the train, the sly hints, suggestions, the way we were always seated next to each other. Other times I was told she needed an escort to the opera or to the theater. It didn't matter to me who I went with; I was fascinated by it all. And, finally, I was trapped. It was the manservant who put laudanum in my glass of champagne. Of course, no one else could have. He poured champagne from the bottle into my glass and somehow added the drug. He and a waiter helped me upstairs and removed my clothes. Eleanor waited until the guests went home and crept into the bed where I was innocently sleeping off the laudanum."

"But, I don't understand, if she didn't want to marry you, why didn't she object?" Winnie Stafford, with her big blue guileless eyes, held her babe in her arms and frowned.

"It was her mother, I think. Fred told her not to go through with it, to sneak out of the church. He had a cab waiting, and they'd leave me standing, red-faced and embarrassed in front of a crowd of people." He laughed bitterly. "But, it didn't work out that way. Her father came for her early, before Fred could put his plan into action. Remember, Fred was a worker; he had duties on the boat. By the time he caught a cab and made it to the church, the vows were made, the congratulations were spoken, the champagne drunk, and I was tied tighter than the harness on a stage coach." They all laughed at the joke. "That's it, except for the ending. I took her the next morning to her parents' house, and she explained her duplicity to her father. While the mother was crying, the father bellowing and the manservant trying to hide his sins, the bride and her lover slipped out the back door and onto a fishing boat bound for Alaska with the outgoing tide."

"What's to be done, now?" That was Walter, always his champion since they were children together, his pretend big brother, his friend.

"It's being done as we speak, Bub." As naturally as breathing, the old childhood name came out. "I went to the bank and made arrangements for the dowry to be returned to the bride's father. He, in his turn, wrote to the mayor and the judge, and quick as a fly is brushed from a mule's behind, the marriage is annulled, I'm free, the bride's on her way to Alaska and only you know what truly happened that night in the hotel room. Who's the guilty party? We were all guilty in our own way, I think." He sat down and put his head in hands. He heard the sound of feet leaving the room. He didn't look up but felt the understanding that surrounded him.

"Fuller. Don't blame yourself. It's a terrible tragedy. But, time will heal the wounds; the pain will recede."

"I know, Papa. But, what about my reputation as a doctor? Will people trust me with their lives after what's being printed in the newspaper? I read one article on the train. It makes me out the darkest villain of all time. They must imagine more than was printed."

"No. I don't think so. I think you'll be the one to receive the sympathy, the compassion."

"How? What are you saying?"

"Think about it without the drama. What did the papers say? The bride left the groom on the day after her wedding and ran off with another man. That's adultery. No matter what they imagine happened in the hotel room, she was the one who ran away from her solemn vows of fidelity and obedience. I'm an old man, son, but the loyalty of a faithful wife is still held sacrosanct in all classes of people. Your mother has left dirty dishes in the kitchen. I think I'll tackle them and go to bed. This is too much for me in one day. Want to help me by drying dishes?"

Fuller saw the situation with clarity for the first time in weeks. "Yes, Papa. I think that's a good idea. If we can't mount the saddle horses and ride into the rain, cleaning the dishes is the best alternative."

Within minutes, Fuller Hadley and his father had the kitchen spotless, and still the rain poured down on the roof of the big house at Sweetwater Springs.

Seventeen

It was just as Joe Hadley, a wise and practical man, prophesied. By the time Fuller returned from his holiday at his parents' farm, the gossip had died down, the commodore and his wife had returned to their home in Alsea Bay in Oregon, the fishing boat had returned with a full load of salmon and the practice of Trifold, Hadley and Smith had a waiting room full of patients. If there were a few wry glances or whispers behind his back, Fuller ignored them. He plunged into the work with a vengeance, spent more time in the slums and tenements, leaving the rich and powerful patients in most cases to his partners, who appreciated the gesture. He still had many contacts with upper society, but it wasn't his main interest. He attended an occasional opera or went to the Palace Hotel for entertainment, but if he was seen on the Barbary Coast, it was usually with his medical bag in hand and his snowy-white coat on his back.

A new Congress was elected and took command of Washington, the Olympic Games were held for the first time in the United States, the excursion steamer *General Slocum* burned in the East River in New York with the loss of over 1,000 persons, and locally, the fishing boats came and went; and on the Fourth of July, 1904, President Theodore Roosevelt sent a message around the world, using a cable from San Francisco to Manila in the Philippines. But, of more importance to Fuller Hadley was the break-up of his long association with his partners, Tom Trifold and Linus Smith.

Linus heard of a small town in Minnesota without a doctor and decided that he'd had enough of the big city life. Tom married and moved to Los Angeles, and Fuller was left with the practice and the responsibilities alike. His bank account was healthy, his hair was beginning to turn gray and his name was known far and wide for his work among the indigent and the wealthy as well. He had more patients than he could handle and hired a doctor straight from medical school to help with the load. Adam Lennox was inexperienced, but he was fully trained and eager to serve. Together, they made a good team, and after a few months, Fuller felt comfortable to visit his folks in Colorado.

It was a good trip; the older children were at schools in the city. Tater and Winnie Stafford had moved into Denver so the children would have a better education, and Fuller was sad that they weren't there to greet him. The saw mill had long since been torn down and almost forgotten. Walter was the overseer of the garden and fields. The animal population had been scaled back to a minimum, and electricity had been strung on wires to the big house and the barn. Fuller knew right away that his mother wasn't well. The years of hard work were beginning to show in her face and her stooping shoulders. Still, there was a bright smile on her scarred face when she greeted him; and her tears flowed as he left.

*****

He returned to his work, refreshed and ready to meet the challenges with boldness and courage. Days turned into weeks, followed by more weeks, and in the next months, Fuller was often called out in the middle of the night to attend a patient.

On one afternoon, Alvord Swanson, a dashing lady-killer of a doctor who had all the nurses swooning with his slicked-down hair and debonair attitude, called to Fuller as he dropped his black bag on the floor in the doctor's receiving room.

"Heh, Hadley, don't you ever check your mail? Looks like a letter in the slot." Indeed, to the side was a rack of pigeon holes of darkened and battered wood with staff names attached, and Fuller's had a thick envelope inside stacked on a number of folded sheaves of paper.

"Some of us have doctoring-type things to do, unlike you ladies' men who flaunt their charm all over the wards. Me? I've just gotten back from San Rosa where that trolley car turned over and injured ten people. I'll pick up my mail when I finish my report and take a shower. Thanks."

Swanson laughed as he pulled on his white coat. "Fine. Thought it might be important information." Just before he opened the door to exit the room, he looked at Fuller with a gleam in his eye, and he chuckled. "Besides, I'm not the ladies' man all the girls are after." Swanson gave him a wave and went on down the hallway toward the women's ward, letting the door swing shut, rattling the bottle glass insert when the latch softly caught.

Fuller made his way to the dining facilities, ate a meal of ham and eggs, stopped by the pharmacy to replace his supply of bandages for his medical bag and picked up his mail. He was surprised to see the letter was in his brother's handwriting. He ducked into an empty patient's room and tore it open.

"Dear Fuller. We were very nearly in need of your skills some days back. There was some manner of excitement down by the corrals when Rose inadvertently got into the pen with Bluenose. The big brute of a bull chased her, and I was forced, at peril to myself, to rush in and grab her. She'd frozen in fear as the bull snorted and pawed the ground in warning of what he intended to do. Thankfully, Brother, we were both able to get out with no injuries. The bull seems no worse for the incident, and we haven't put him down for it. We expect several new calves in the spring, a boon for the farm, as we can sell them or have meat in a year or two, if they grow as fast as the last set did.

"You may remember the storm that came through while you were here last. Another hit, but worse. The roof of the goat shed blew off, and Rufus Blackburn, the new hired hand, repaired the roof. It hasn't leaked since, which makes him a man handy to have around.

"Papa became angrier than I've ever seen him. Noah had taken the bow from the wall, and in playing with it, it was broken. However, Papa applied a little glue and wrapped the place with rawhide, and it now hangs on the wall once again.

"Vanessa received a letter from her father saying his wife lost a leg due to an infection. Vanessa and I agree that Capt. Zalman will need additional help, and she's decided to go to Kansas to take care of her mother. I'll join her later, along with the children.

"Signed: Your brother, Johnie."

"Kansas, huh, that's a long ways. Papa will miss them. Wonder who'll take care of Vanessa's roses?" Fuller stuffed the letter in the pocket of his white coat and left the room. He had duties to perform, and he needed time to absorb the import of his brother's words.

He stopped by Mr. Springer's room, intending to speak with him of the man's favorite sports team, the New York Highlanders. Springer knew the team's history, back to their origin as the Baltimore Orioles, with a winning tradition in the '90s. There was some talk of renaming the team the Yankees, and he wanted the man's opinion, but he was distracted by the thought of his little brother leaving for Kansas. He signed the form allowing Springer to be released from the hospital the next day and was out the door before he remembered to bring up the Highlanders. He stopped by the nurses' station and gave the nurse on duty instructions on Jeffry Belmont, who had come in with a knife wound. With his hospital duties completed, Fuller left for afternoon office hours with Adam back at their clinic.

He was surprised to find Adam in the entrance hall to their combined office and home as he made his way through the front door. The man's face bore a sheen of sweat, even though it was mid-winter.

"You gotta get you one of these." Adam held a bicycle in

his hands, and he leaned it against the stair railing as he pulled a cloth from his back pocket to wipe his forehead. "This is the best mode of transportation in the city, the wisest investment I've made in a long time."

"Nah, my man, you ride, if you want. I'll take the trolley." Fuller laughed as he walked through, heading to the surgery. No patients were scheduled until the afternoon hours, and this was his chance to organize any materials that had inadvertently been left out the day before. Sharing the surgery with his partner meant that sometimes one man thought the other needed equipment out and available, when it was simply overlooked from a previous consultation.

"No, seriously, Fuller." Adam came up behind him, tossing one arm over Fuller's shoulders. "Look at me, fit as a fiddle." He slapped his own stomach, and it made a hollow sound.

"Hungry and skinny is more like it." Fuller shrugged the arm off. "This is San Francisco. What do you do when you come to hills? Oh, wait, you get off and walk. Why do you need a bike if you're going to walk, anyway?"

"Can't convince you, huh?" Adam pushed at his shoulder, and as he turned away, he used his cloth to wipe at the back of his neck, tossing it carelessly onto a small console table when he was finished and taking his bike in hand to carry it up the stairs.

The bicycle provided a moment of hilarity, however. One morning in late March, the weather turned, and the fog filled the bay with ghostly fingers stretching into the streets fronting the water. The two men took some time to make their way to Golden Gate Park, as there had been recent reports of whales in the harbor. They also hoped to see a tall-masted sailing ship, for several had come in during the previous weeks and were of a special interest to Fuller. Adam rode his treasured bicycle, and Fuller traveled on one of the city's ubiquitous trolleys. On the way, Adam was on the bike, riding uphill, and peddling furiously to try to keep up with the trolley. Of course, he fell farther and farther behind. Fuller stood aboard, one hand holding to a rail, and leaning out, yelled encouragement.

"Come, man, you can do it. Peddle harder!"

"It's all I've got!" Adam barely got the words out. He was standing, and the bike shifted from side to side as he forced his legs to put the maximum amount of energy into each turn of the crank.

Reaching the apex of the hill was when the situation really ramped up. The trolley slowed, preparing to disgorge the passengers who wanted off, allowing Adam to regain the distance lost. Fuller stepped off, calling, "Always bringing up the rear. You couldn't come in first if you wanted, you cad, you!" He raised a hand to wave.

About then, Adam also raised a hand, but his fingers were twisted to express a vulgar sentiment, although he had a laugh on his face as he did so, and it was clear the obscenity was in jest. He paused in his peddling, only to have his pants leg twist into the spokes of the rear wheel, locking up the mechanism. He paused as if frozen for about ten seconds, his bike precariously balanced, then he crashed to the side, barely missing a woman stepping out of a shop who wore a fashionable skirt that just exposed her ankles, showing leather shoes with high tops and contrasting buttons up one side. She carried several packages in her hands, and they went flying.

When Fuller got to him, laughing until he felt the temperature had gone up ten degrees, he reached his hand out. "If you could've seen your face. You looked as if you'd seen a ghost."

"Seen a ghost? I thought it had my bike and was shaking me off." Adam released Fuller's hand and brushed at his clothes. They helped the woman collect her packages, and Adam inspected the bike to find it was undamaged in any serious way, but his pants were less well off. One leg had severe grease marks, although it didn't seem to be torn.

The weather was so improved by the early weeks in April that the two men had taken to spending some time outdoors or visiting clubs with their beaus or chums of the moment, often staying out until the early hours of the morning. A recent song that Fuller especially liked was *Anchors Aweigh*, a rousing medley that he would often sing loudly after visiting a drinking establishment.

"This man, he thinks he's a Caruso." Adam jabbed Charlie Zonders, an occasional buddy of theirs, in the side, nodding at Fuller, holding to a lamp post, and at that moment, changing to *You're a Grand Old Flag*, a current hit directly from New York that had become popular after opening in a play the previous month.

"Aye, he's quite good after a few pints of ale, to my ears anyway." Charlie joined in on the chorus, creating a ruckus that was less improvement than cacophonous accompaniment.

An irate man on the fourth floor of a neighboring building didn't agree with Charlie's assessment. He leaned out in the darkness, yelling about it being near midnight, and slamming the window closed when he drew back inside.

Adam never quite got the two men quieted, and in fact joined in as they switched to *Dill Pickles Rag*, a favorite of his, but there were no more incidences of disturbed sleepers, at least that they were aware of.

In spite of that, the sleeping arrangements of most of the city's inhabitants were rudely disrupted a few days later, although it had nothing to do with Fuller's singing abilities.

The episodes of the earth shaking were familiar to the people of the City by the Bay, but on April 18, 1906, the most devastating earthquake on record hit the city of San Francisco, and Fuller was plunged into the midst of the disaster. He'd been out the night before with Adam and his date, Myrna Golden, and a ravishing blonde named Cleva Nevin, wearing a scant lacy frock of pink. They separated shortly after midnight, and Fuller held Cleva tightly while they staggered up the three flights of stairs to her apartment. She was singing one of the popular ragtime songs they had heard at the party.

"Shh, you'll wake the neighbors," Fuller tried to warn her. He had his reputation to think about.

She laughed, "Shh, neighbors, it's me. Don't wake up, you'll frighten my fellow. He's a doctor." She almost fell, and Fuller caught her just in time as they staggered against the wall. She unlocked the door, and they fell laughing onto the bed, arms and legs tangled. Fuller felt slightly nauseous as he scrambled to remove his trousers. The pink frock fell on the floor, and Cleva moaned with pleasure as he plunged into her. They fell asleep drunk; damp and sated.

He heard and felt the quake in the early morning hours and

rose from the bed while it was moving and shaking. He had to hold the bedpost as he searched in the dark for his trousers.

"Honey, what's wrong? Oh, my God, it's an earthquake." Cleva screamed and threw the covers over her head as a picture fell to the floor with a shower of glass.

"Get dressed," Fuller demanded. "You have to go outside." He was having trouble buttoning his pants as the second shock hit. He heard the thump of footsteps racing down the stairs and the thunder of plaster falling in the room above them. He ran to the closet nook and pulled out a dress and threw it on the bed. "Here, put this on and hurry." He looked around for his medical bag and grabbed the handle with relief.

"That old thing? I never wear that. It's ugly." She jumped out of bed and crawled under it. She screamed when he pulled her out by the leg.

"You can't stay here. Come on, woman; the roof may fall in. Get dressed," he bellowed, and she began to pull her clothes on, fear in her eyes.

"I have to go to the hospital. Grab your handbag and coat and get out of the building. Go to the park, but don't stand under any trees. Stay in the open. Goodbye." He almost made it to the door.

She yanked on his arm. "Don't leave me alone, Honey. I can't be alone." He shrugged her off, and holding tight to his medical bag, he left her there. The sound of panicked people screaming, shattering of glass and falling bricks and mortar were everywhere. He cautiously rushed past a gaping hole in one street and found the hospital slightly damaged but the surgery intact.

He worked for hours repairing wounded bodies and mending broken bones; the surgeons took whatever case came to them, no matter the class of the person or the injury. Many died, and he had no time to mourn. He barely had time to dictate to a nurse or orderly the name, the date and the cause of death. Inside the hospital, frantic orderlies ran to and fro pushing the carriages of the dead and dying along the corridors and into the operating theater. The stench of human flesh and toxic fumes penetrated the walls as Fuller took a short break with Adam in the dining facilities to eat and catch up on the news.

A doctor rushed past them, his clothing smelling of gas, and his face pale with shock. Another, a man Fuller recognized but couldn't put a name to, paused, still pulling his smock over his civilian clothes. He stepped to Fuller's and Adam's table.

"Doctor Marin, obstetrics. I've seen you around but never got the chance to introduce myself. Dr. Hadley, I believe, and you're Adam Lennox." He gave a rough chuckle and held out his hand. "I was at an event celebrating my uncle and aunt's 50th. It was just winding down when all hell broke loose. Of course, the women had all gone home, so it was just the men left, thank God. We were able to get into the street before the ceiling fell in. Dozens would have been killed otherwise."

Fuller shook the proffered hand, asking, "How are things holding up outside?"

"Fires everywhere, from broken gas mains, I overheard a crew talking. You can hear it spewing out when you pass wrecked houses. One man was lighting a smoke, and he tossed his match onto a pile of rubble. It exploded as I watched, throwing him down and catching his hair on fire. We were lucky to get him away before he was burned badly."

"It's as awful as all that?" Adam's eyes were wide.

"Worse," Marin assured him. "Once a building starts to burn, there's nothing to be done. There's so many broken water lines that nothing can be put out."

Fuller stood, unable to imagine the terror and devastation, in spite of what he'd seen as he made his way to the hospital. He watched through the door as nurses and doctors rushed past, several with nightclothes showing beneath their hospital smocks. Occasionally one stepped through the door, trading places with someone leaving. Through a broken window, sporadic sirens filtered in, supporting Marin's statement. It seemed the entire city would be gone before the day was done.

"Dr. Marin?" An orderly appeared at the door. One side of his face was smeared with soot, and his hair was in disarray. "It's Mrs. Weintraub. It seems her baby isn't waiting until next week as you'd predicted."

"Fine, fine. I'm on my way." Marin took a deep breath and smiled over-broadly. He nodded in farewell to Fuller and Adam, calling out, "Doctors," and walked toward the doors.

"Bedlam. That's what it'll be." Fuller said the words to himself as much as anyone.

Marin stopped at the door, looking back, and responded to the comment. "Not will be. Is. The Army's been called out to stop the looting and to help the wounded, but I'm not sure what can be done at this point."

"The Army?" An intern Fuller knew only as Jonsy was sitting with his head in his hands, and he looked up, his expression haggard. "Are we to be under martial law?"

"Looting? That's all people can think about? The fools! What could be important enough to steal, when lives are being lost?" asked an older doctor, whom Fuller had seen often on his rounds. He didn't remember his name.

Fuller looked around the room and heard the muttering of many voices. A clatter nearby distracted him as a nurse started to rise, her arm brushing the dishes from the table, and she fell to the floor.

"Here," he called out. "Someone get a carriage." He took her pulse and raised one eyelid. "She'll be alright," he said to the orderlies who rushed up with a gurney. "See if you can find an empty bed and let her sleep."

"I don't think there are any empty beds." Adam quietly spoke at his elbow. He turned to the men who were lifting the woman onto the carriage. "Take her to the nurses' lounge."

But, the woman was beginning to wake. She sat up, and embarrassed, stepped down from the carriage. Two of her companions helped her from the room. The orderlies took the carriage away.

Adam laughed. "Well, that eased the talk of looting. What do you think, Fuller?"

"I don't have time to think, partner. I'm going back to the fourth floor operating room. I'll see you when I can." He marched out of the room, leaving Adam to dispose of their trays and empty dishes.

Fuller treated so many burns that he lost count. Sometime during the first night, they were told the hospital was being evacuated, and that tents were set up in Ingleside and North Beach. As they were packing up some of their most sensitive equipment, Petey Farquhar, a surgeon new to the hospital, a man with a tall, lanky physique and uncontrollable tawny hair, caught Fuller on the arm.

"What bothers me, Fuller, is there's no local newspapers. How are we supposed to know what's happening?" Petey's face was haggard, and his stained smock showed the hours he'd been hard at work trying to help the injured.

"I've heard that the newspapers in San Rosa have loaned the printers space in their plant until they can replace their equipment and newsprint. Must have been a mighty big fire to burn all that paper." Fuller laughed, but no one laughed with him. Petey shook his head, giving little more than a false chuckle. The man's eyes were reddened with the elevated exhaustion of the long hours spent and still left to spend before the city could return to a semblance of order.

In the silence, Fuller became aware of the callous nature of his joke, and embarrassed, he left the room.

He took a few hours to eat, sleep and bathe at one of the volunteer shelters and headed for Ingleside, where he heard the cries of the orphans and the mothers who had lost their children, mended the injured and prayed with the mourning. On the fourth day he could no longer stand, he was so tired, and his body so ripe that he couldn't abide the smell of his own person. He saw from a distance the raging fires and heard the sound of the dynamite used to lessen the damage, but he knew even if it was rebuilt, San Francisco would never be as it was when he had arrived as a wide-eyed physician fresh from the wonders of Europe and his peaceful home in the mountains.

He took a full twenty-four hours to rebuild his strength and returned to the fray; again, he worked until exhausted, and knowing that others would take his place, he took the ferry to Oakland and rented a single room with bath in the city. Along the way, he visited a newspaper vendor on the street hawking papers from various cities. Although the earthquake had decimated the newspaper printing facilities in San Francisco itself, news sheets from as far away as the Central Plains had begun to arrive in the city. There were current editions of papers from Los Angeles and Sacramento, and he selected one of each, but several old copies stacked at the back showing Colorado Springs and Denver caught his eyes. He was hungry for the news, and Colorado made him wonder what his parents were reading of the quake. He paid for the papers and made his way to his room.

He sat with the papers spread over the bed and on the floor. A half-filled glass of whiskey formed a ring on the bedside table. Fuller's hair was tousled, his face was pale and his hands coated with ink from the papers. He pulled up the Colorado Springs *Daily Gazette*. The April 21 edition was headlined, "Scene after shock one of wild confusion." And do I know it, Fuller thought. I was there. What am I thinking? I *am* there.

He thought of his parents, realizing they would have read the reports as well. He pulled out a sheaf of paper and an ink pen, and he jotted a quick note he would put in the post the first opportunity he got.

"I am well but exhausted. I was with a friend when the city seemed to come down around us. I escaped with my clothes and my medical bag. I am in a room in Oakland, which is mostly undamaged from the quake. My medical skills are needed, as there are more injured than what we can relieve of their suffering. Signed: Your son, Fuller."

He set the letter aside and thought of Cleva. He'd need to search her out. Surely she was alright, but he couldn't worry about what he had no control over.

Fuller caught up on the back issues of additional newspapers, and was disarmed totally to find the Palace Hotel had burned, the mansion of Commodore Fallon in which he'd celebrated his engagement was nothing but rubble and a whole six blocks around his apartment building had been destroyed.

"San Francisco in ruins; Pacific Coast in Panic as fires sweep through the city; A possible 1,000 dead, many more homeless; Damage estimated at $200,000,000; Officials call out troops to quall the looting; Flames spread to residential districts; Sanford University destroyed.

"At last count, maybe 20,000 refuges roaming the streets struggling to get out of the rubble; One lady seen wandering with a bird cage in her hand; Dead horses litter the street and danger of disease runs high."

"Canons trained on the homes of millionaires in vain effort to staunch the all-consuming flames."

"All citizens of the town are saddened to hear of the destruction of some of the city's finest mansions. Ladies still dressed in their finery and furs were seen carrying precious family pets from their homes before the dynamite was set that would leave them homeless. Small children holding tightly to their mother's hands and servants scrambled to bring out what they could save of their possessions."

Fuller's eyes were caught by a column titled: Partial List of

Dead. He ran his finger down the column and saw two of his former patients: John Turner, fish market, Montgomery and Sacramento Streets, and T. L. Alchord, 52, Stevenson Street. His finger stopped and his heart skipped a beat at the sight that swam before his eyes: Cleva Nevin, 24, Williams Street.

Lovely, vivacious Cleva; she had been in his arms only moments before the quake. He reached for the glass, drank the whiskey, and poured another drink from the bottle. Holding the amber liquid in his shaking hand, he gazed out the small window. In the distance, he could see black smoke hovering over the city. He raised the glass to his lips and felt the liquid burn his throat as he swallowed. After a few moments, he went back to the list: Percival Broderick, Valencia Hotel; William Filbert, injured by falling walls and died at the Mechanics pavilion; Irene Pennell, 72, mortally cut by glass, Mechanics pavilion.

He had to turn aside at the bitter sting of tears when he saw her name. He shut his eyes, and he could clearly see in his mind the slender, sober-faced woman, dressed in a dark gray dress, white apron and white cap on her head, which totally covered her hair. She had taken care of Tom Trifold, Linus Smith and himself as though they were small, recalcitrant boys given into her care.

He moved his finger on down the list, determined to see them all; Dr. Alvord Swanson, 32, well-known young physician killed in his room on the seventh floor of the California hotel. He remembered Alvord; they had played poker several times with his friends Tom and Linus. He could see him in his head, frowning when he had a bad hand. Finally, at the end of the list were those who had not been identified: three Chinese, two unknown white women, an unknown sailor in uniform, all found on Hayes and Polk Streets, and unknown man, Wilcox Street. His eyes saw a small square advertisement that said: "Special offerings on pianos," and below were the prices and makes. The absurdity of the small bid for sales set him to laughing. He put the paper away and sat in his chair until he could calm himself. Lifting his first letter, he decided he could phrase it better now that he was thinking clearly. He wadded it, rose from his chair, and retrieved paper and pen to write his father.

"Dear Papa: I am alive and well. I was in the St. Francis hotel when the quake hit and have lost all my personal effects except my medical bag, the suit I am wearing and my hat. I have done what I could to relieve the suffering of the poor and needy; so many dead and wounded. I can be reached for the next few weeks at the address below or at the hospital listed below. Pray for us all. I will stay until the worst of the tragedy is over. Your loving and obedient son, Fuller."

He rose the next morning and, after dropping the letter into the slot at the post office, he visited the bank, hoping he could sort out his bank account, but was told it might take weeks, as their records in San Francisco were burned. He applied for insurance on his possessions in the apartment and was given no assurance that it would be available for him.

He received a loan from hospital staff on his salary for the month, enough to pay expenses and a ticket to Colorado, and after two days, returned to the tent city, where he helped the other doctors and often took the duties of nurse, bathing a man's face, emptying a woman's bedpan, changing dressings on the seriously burned. He saw and heard more cries for help than during his years in the Navy; he smelled the rotting flesh of humans and animals alike; and long after the turmoil was over, he could still hear the clanging of the fire wagons in his mind if not his ears.

In the city, the water lines and gas mains were repaired, the Army returned to the Presidio, and lumber, bricks and glass began to once again take the form of houses and business enterprises. Fuller followed the officials and staff of the hospital as they moved from place to place until a permanent hospital could be built. He heard the rumors of corruption and graft, but since they didn't directly affect him, he ignored them. His whole world, as never before, was centered on the care of the injured people.

He heard of a clothing store selling their goods at half price, and he bought a suit, a couple of shirts and some undergarments with part of his dwindling funds, and visited a tonsorial parlor; but even with the smell of spice and pomade on his hair, he couldn't seem to shake the scent of rotting flesh about him. If he occasionally took a weekend to gamble and visit the dancing halls and brothels, he told himself it was his due.

At last, on the first day of August, Fuller Hadley took the ferry from San Francisco to Oakland and caught the train to Colorado. He was pleased to learn the line now had a dining car, although he couldn't imagine how they would prepare meals on a moving train. He stopped his porter as he carried Fuller's luggage to his compartment.

"Are meals served in our compartments, or do passengers dress for dinner?" He had suitable clothing, but only just. It was all packed, however.

"Sir, you haven't ridden with us in some time, I suppose. We have a car set up as fine as any restaurant you'll ever have chance to visit." The porter smiled.

"And a kitchen? You have a kitchen on a train?" Fuller shook his head, astonished at the new amenities since his last trip to Colorado.

"Here's a menu, sir." The porter reached in his jacket and held a card out to Fuller. "Make a selection. I have to turn it in ahead of time. It's easiest if I take it now, although if you need some time, I can return when the other passengers are settled."

"Nah, let me have a look." Fuller lifted the shade and held the card close to the glass. He read off, "Pan fried rainbow trout, oxtail, and fresh fruit. You have fresh fruit aboard?" One of the varieties listed was strawberries. He lowered the card, amazed that they would have fresh strawberries aboard.

"Yes, sir, and wine and whiskey, if you feel the inclination. Do you wish to make your choice now, or would you prefer me to return in a few minutes?"

"Trout, with plenty of whiskey, and some of those strawberries."

"Yes, sir. I'll mark that down." The porter chuckled, wrote down his choice, tipped his hat, and backed out of the compartment, stuffing a bill Fuller gave him into his pocket.

The dining car impressed Fuller. He'd not expected linen tablecloths, crystal, and fresh flowers. He sat across from a mature woman wearing her hair on top of her head. She had a blue silk ribbon worked into the effusive mass with a feather dancing to the side. She wore a matching dress, with ribbons in a contrasting yellow woven through stitching around the collar and cuffs. Huge pockets adorned the lower half, with silver buttons resembling dollar coins on the flaps. They introduced themselves.

"Good evening, sir. Mrs. Annette Crompton, traveling across the country to enjoy the various artists exhibiting in the modern style." She said it with a smile, holding out her hand

"Ah, Monet." He stood and took her hand, placing it to his lips in the French style.

"More importantly, Degas. You've heard of him, I'm certain." Annette seated herself with a flourish.

"Let me think." Fuller frowned. "Dancers, with lots of light?"

"You've seen his work, then. I do so love his presentation of color. Magnificent. Ah, there's my daughter." A younger female, quite plain, came to the table, kissed the older woman on the cheek and sat beside Fuller. She wore a dark-blue sailor-style dress with a large collar, white trim, and white repeated at the cuffs of the sleeves. A pronounced row of buttons trailed down the front. Her hair was loosely fluffed on top of her head.

"Mama, who's your dining companion?" She glanced at Fuller, but didn't speak to him or look directly at him.

"Dr. Hadley, my dear. Lately from San Francisco. Introduce yourself."

She turned to Fuller. "Jewell Hinckley. I suppose you're leaving all that destruction behind." She shuddered.

"Did you know someone in the city?" Fuller nodded politely.

"I would like you to change the subject, Dr. Hadley. What

destination do you have in mind?"

Fuller told her briefly of his parents' home in Colorado. Before long Jewell seemed to lose interest, and he turned to Mrs. Crompton and enjoyed a lively discussion of the characteristics and merits of Degas' distinctive style of work. The food arrived, Fuller's trout on a bed of rice, with mushrooms, leeks and asparagus on the side. The women had roasted chicken, with toasted bread and a side of salad. Fuller asked if they minded if he took his whiskey, and Jewell assured him it was his business, although she personally considered the stuff to be a vile distraction to the purer pursuits available to modern man. Mrs. Crompton sniffed when the whiskey arrived, but she didn't criticize Fuller other than that. Fuller enjoyed the discussion about art, but his impression of the women was one of embittered females who made a poor evening's company.

With the meal completed, Fuller thanked the women for their acquaintance and made his way to the smoking car in an attempt to find someone of better company. He introduced himself to a portly gentleman who wanted to talk only of himself and the killing he'd made on buying up vacated lots in the razed parts of San Francisco and reselling them at a profit to builders striving to meet the desperate demand for new housing. Fuller soon grew bored, as there were no current newspapers, and the other men were engrossed in their own lives and seemed disinterested in beginning stimulating conversation. He made his way to his quarters to find the porter had turned down the bed. Gratefully, he stripped off his clothes, donned striped, silk pajamas, and fell onto the soft linens, and was soon fast asleep.

It was a completely different man from the one who had

traveled to California over a decade before who stepped from the train into the clear, cool air of his mountain roots. He was met at the station by Tater and Winnie Stafford, and the smiling face of his childhood friend and brother-in-law, Walter Abernathy. They stayed for the night with Tater and their children. He found it soothing to sit and talk of ordinary things, the weather, the local news, politics, and books and plays they had read or seen. There were rumors of a fleet of U. S. Navy ships traveling around the world, but Walter brushed it off as what it was, rumors.

The next morning after an early breakfast, Walter and Fuller left for the farm. They talked sporadically, as old friends do, and as the late afternoon sun was half-hidden by the forest, Fuller began to feel more energetic and joyful than he had in a long time. With an instinct that welled up from years of active service to the sick and helpless, Fuller knew that he would never return to San Francisco. There was nothing left for him there. He and Adam would terminate the partnership, and if he could persuade his friend to come to Colorado, he would use his part of the monetary value to open a practice in Denver, high in the mountains, where he would tend the poor of his homeland. If Adam couldn't be persuaded, he'd ask another young future-leaning physician to join him.

As Walter drove into the yard, he knew what to expect and watch for; his beloved mother was extremely ill. He hadn't been told until last night at the Stafford home, because they knew he was needed in California. He went directly to the big white house and was met by his father, pale, withdrawn and not at all his usual charming, cheerful self. They spent a few minutes quietly talking and went upstairs to the bedroom. The signs were all there, and Fuller read them well. Janey got up from her chair beside the bed and gave him a hug, and he turned to the sleeping woman in the bed. He took her wrist and listened to the pulse. He opened his bag and listened to her heart, and he stepped out into the hallway and went downstairs with his grieving father.

"Papa, it's bad, but you already know that. I'd say a couple of weeks, maybe a month on the optimistic side. I can give her something to ease the pain if she's suffering, and I'll be here for her if she needs me. I have no home in San Francisco; it was destroyed in the fires. I have sufficient funds in the bank to last for years. Adam and I are dissolving the partnership. I'll look around and see about opening a clinic in Denver. But, for the time being, I'm home to stay. No more roaming and rambling for me." He smiled, hoping his father would feel more cheerful, but it was a sad, sorrowful man who hugged his son with tears glistening in his eyes and went back upstairs to where his heart was.

Eighteen

As though the sun rejoiced at the return of the Prodigal Son, it shone with a bright yellow glow over the farmland carved from the wilderness, among the pines and spruce, the cotton-woods and the willows. Walter showed Fuller the improvements since he was there last, and they rode the horses over the land. They talked of many things, and Fuller was able to reacquaint himself with his sister. Only the youngest children, the bright-eyed Gloria, the studious Noah, and the rambunctious John, now five and the image of his father, still lived at home in the old station house, with the two older boys away at school. At thirteen, Gloria was turning into a beauty like her mother, but unlike her mother, there was no hint of mothering instinct, not in the skirts and painted nails sort of way. Fuller had yet to see her in a dress since returning, and she kept her hair in a knot at the base of her neck or tied with a scarf. Fuller was amused at his niece's antics, for she rode a horse and herded the cattle like a man. One day, he was out among the outbuildings, and he heard her voice yell out.

"Noah, put that book down and help me wrangle this calf."

"Sis, Arthur is just about to rescue Lancelot."

"Now, brother!"

Fuller stepped around the end of the barn to see the two in a corral, and three calves running free. Gloria stood over the fourth, and she was tying its legs with a length of cord. A thick book was carelessly leaned against one of the fence posts. Fuller picked it up and recognized *King Arthur and the Knights of the Round Table*. It was a little more battered than he remembered, but it was clearly the same. He thumbed through to a few favorite passages, laughed and laid it back where the boy had left it.

"Niece, nephew," Fuller called. "How's it going with the calves?"

"Fine, Uncle Fuller." Gloria drew herself erect, and she waved. Stepping away from the calf, she put her hand to her mouth and whistled sharply and loudly. The calf twisted and tried to get up, but it tumbled back down every time. "Noah, another cord. I've got three more calves to hogtie."

Fuller laughed and stepped away. That was a girl he could appreciate. She was a replica of her father, and Fuller was reminded of the days when it was he and Bub who rode through the grass and the corn rows on one of the mustangs.

Sometimes Janey came to prepare a meal, but Fuller was surprised to see a housekeeper had taken over the duties of the kitchen. Her name was Corinne Stapleton, but everyone called her Corey. She was a middle-age widow who had been found by Winnie at a homeless shelter in Denver. Offered a position in the forest and a permanent home if she wanted it, she grabbed at the chance. She was a good cook, but her specialty was a frozen pudding. They all complained they'd gain weight, but with electricity in the house, ice was available year round, and on a hot, August afternoon, the treat was welcome.

Over the next weeks, Fuller slipped effortlessly into the household routines. He selected a room in which to sleep; sorted out his few possessions, transferring them into one of the empty bedrooms; made himself at home in the gardens and slowed down to the pace of life on the farm. Books were taken off the shelves and reread before the window.

Fuller spent hours with his mother, reading to her, talking to her and praying for her. He tried to be a loving son, not a doctor, but his trained eyes could see the daily wasting away, her puckered, scarred face so pale it was almost translucent.

"Fuller?" Her voice was weak but spirited. "Where's Joe?" She looked around the room.

"He stepped to the barn to see the new colt, Mama. He's a lovely chestnut, strong and healthy, Bub says. Do you want me to call Papa?" He kept all emotion from his face as he'd been trained to do with terminally ill patients.

"No, son, leave him be. Has he named the colt?"

Fuller took his mother's blue-veined, calloused hand in his own soft, manicured one. He could see a few scars from burns she had suffered while cooking hundreds of meals on the old wood-burning kitchen range.

"I think he named him Lancelot. He was one of the Knights of the Round Table, you know."

Hannah smiled and fell asleep, her slightly gray hair

streaming over the pillow. Fuller sat silently beside the bed and watched her chest move slowly up and down. He placed her hand at her side and pulled the covers over her shoulders. She moaned but didn't stir.

Three weeks past the date of his arrival, Hannah Hadley, pioneer and partner, wife, mother and grandmother passed quietly and courageously from one great adventure into the next. Johnie and Vanessa, Janey and Walter, the boy she had cared for most of his life, and Fuller, her first-born, and most of the grandchildren were nearby when she closed her eyes to sleep. Joe was devastated, and he wept. Fuller took over as physician and did what was necessary, and she was laid to rest under the fallen pine needles next to her stillborn daughter, Anne.

Joe took himself to task and did the eulogy. Still tall and handsome, he told again the story of when he and Hannah were children; how he had loved her, although he didn't realize it until he was forced to take a wife in order to have the position as station manager at Sweetwater Creek. He told of her bravery and her graciousness to the passengers, the coachmen and the animal handlers. He had to stop a minute as Walter blew his nose loudly in his handkerchief, and everyone knew how he had come as a child of ten with his father Roland as animal handler to take the place of Slim, the veterinarian. It was cool among the pines, and a gentle breeze caused a few pine cones to clatter to the ground as Joe ended his eulogy, speaking of the pride Hannah had felt in her children and her grandchildren. The silence was unsettling, and everyone looked at him as he murmured, "Good night, my darling wife; sleep well."

He turned and walked into the forest, but no one worried about him, for he'd been hunting in those trees for most of his life and knew every path and boulder.

Fuller and the rest of the family returned to the house. Corey fixed a tasty meal, and everyone sat around the large dining table as they always did when together. Plans were made for Johnie and Vanessa and the children to return to their home. Tater and Winnie drove back to Denver, and there were only Fuller and Walter left to drive the wagon to the river and choose a rounded stone to carve the name and dates of Hannah Hadley on the rock. Joe watched them from the shade of a cottonwood tree and listened to the ground squirrels and the birds singing in the trees. Fuller sat with him after Walter went to his home in the old station house.

"Papa, how do you stand the quiet?"

"Quiet? It's not quiet, Fuller. Can't you hear them? The sound of hooves splashing through the creek and pounding on the ground, covered with dust and manure; the creak of the harness; the sound of old Rusty Backgammon's trumpet and his loud curses, and Grover and Paul and Manning, Jim and Fizzure; Buck and Rosie, and Slim and Roland's clanging of the hammer on the anvil; Jack's barking, the neighing of the horses, the sound of the goats, and the cluck of chickens, and the soft, gentle rain on the roof. No, Fuller, it's not quiet here. It's peaceful." Joe Hadley smiled at his son, and Fuller understood. Since the experience of the last weeks, he knew a peace so dear, so precious that he wondered why he hadn't noticed it before.

"Papa, you're right. It's not quiet; it's peaceful. May it ever be so."

"Amen." They sat quietly talking until the sun was gone and the flying insects drove them into the house. The stars came out, and the moon was lifted into the sky and gazed down on the land as it had since it was created. A gentle breeze blew through the treetops, and the sound of a coyote was heard in the distance.

Nineteen

Fuller Hadley remained at Sweetwater Springs. He opened a free clinic for the indigent in Denver and worked four days a week, giving his services to all who needed a physician without asking for payment. His funds were at last transferred from the bank in San Francisco to Denver, and he received a handsome settlement from the insurance company for the loss of his possessions when the apartment house was destroyed. A portion of the money was used to establish living quarters for the time each week he would spend in the city. Fuller searched out a new housekeeper to join him, and they took up residence in the apartment. Her name was Girtie Longfellow, a spinster who had lived with her brother until his death in the war in '98. Fuller sympathized with her, well aware the man might have been on the island of Cuba, suffering from debilitating malaria, even as Fuller enjoyed the sweet ocean breezes aboard his ship. He considered that his time in the Navy might have been much worse had he not gained such a providential berth aboard the

Oregon. The remainder of the money established a foundation in the names of Josiah and Hannah Hadley, and the funds used to pay salaries and the expenses necessary for running the clinic.

His friend Adam Lennox wanted to remain in San Francisco, so Fuller found another physician who wanted his own practice, but couldn't afford the high cost of medical equipment or the mortgage of a building. His name was Septimus Roman because he was the seventh in a family of fourteen. He joined the clinic staff the next year, along with his wife, Philbertha, called Philly, an experienced surgical nurse. They lived in a modest house near the clinic but visited the farm as time would permit.

Girtie soon picked up on one of Hannah's favorite recipes from Fuller's sister, Janey, who shared her father's favorites. Girtie became quite proficient at preparing the fruit pocket pies Hannah had created so long ago to satisfy the travelers coming through on the stages. One afternoon, when Fuller was especially hungry, he came down the stairs, drawn by the intense aroma of apples.

"Girtie?" He called his housekeeper's name as he reached the downstairs landing. "I smell pies. Apple?"

"Aye, sir, and they's being for the evening meal, so you keeps yours hands off." She appeared at the kitchen door, a red-checked apron covering her ample girth, and wiping her hands on a flour-strewn kitchen cloth. "They be cooling off, and I know the ones I made. I be missing any, and I'll know wheres they've gone." She nodded severely at him, but there was a wink, too.

220

Fuller caught the wink, and he was pretty sure there was an extra just for him. When he heard Girtie next, he knew he was right.

"I'm stepping out to the line to hang my kitchen cloths, Dr. Hadley. I'll be back in five minutes, you count my word. Remember, the pies are cooling as I speak."

The screen door slammed, and Fuller made his way to the kitchen. As he expected, there sat a number of the small pies, laid out neatly to cool. One was just off to the side, slightly separated from the rest, given the extra space to cool more quickly. Fuller snatched it up and put it to his mouth, enjoying the juicy apple filling as it ran down his chin.

"I'm coming in, Doctor. I hope you haven't bothered my pies."

Fuller laughed, and he crammed the last of the pie into his mouth. When Gertie came through the door, she eyed the pies carefully as if counting, then looked at him just as he choked the last of the pie down.

"So, they meet your approval, I sees." She nodded with a smile on her face.

"What?" Fuller held his hands up, palms out, in feigned innocence.

"Good, I made them specially for you. Here, take another." She placed a second pie on a folded cloth and handed it to Fuller, and she shooed him out the door.

When in his forties, Fuller began to feel a nagging pain in his thumbs and the first finger of his left hand whenever he read a heavy book or used his hands in surgery for long periods of time. At first, he rubbed the spot and the pain would lessen; then he began to take medication for the pain. Finally, on a cold, blustery day in early March in the year 1909 when the pain was especially gruesome, he made an appointment to see one of his hospital colleagues.

"Well, Neal, what do you say?" he asked when the examination was finished, and he was sitting across from his friend in his office.

"I 'spect you already know, Fuller. You've probably seen the symptoms before. That's why you came to me. Does rheumatoid arthritis run in your family?" Dr. Neal Champion looked at the young man with sympathy. He was dressed in a dark blue suit, striped shirt with a high white stiff collar and tie. On his feet were shiny leather shoes. Fuller Hadley was a strong, virile man on the outside, but inside was seething with anger and resentment.

"My grandmother had it. She never complained, but she suffered for as long as I can remember. When I was young, I didn't know why she couldn't do certain things with me, like throw a ball or help me stack my blocks. I took it as natural." He looked past the doctor toward a window and saw the building across the street. "She was my dear grandmother; I loved her the way she was."

"Hummph." Neal brought his attention back to the booklined room with the framed medical certificates on the wall. "I'd say, five, maybe ten years, if you're lucky, before the bone erosion and damage to the cartilage prevent you from working. It's a heavy blow for a man of your talent and experience to lose your ability to function as a surgeon; but there are other fields: teaching, lecturing. You could even hire a secretary and write a book." He laughed, but Fuller didn't join him.

He stood, walked around the desk and shook the doctor's hand. "Thanks, Neal, I'll consider what you say. Maybe I'll be a famous author, a font of wisdom for the medical students of America." He smiled and left the room, his shoulders slumped and his face so fierce, one of the patients waiting to see Dr. Champion cringed in his chair.

He walked to his office and continued with his day, but his heart was heavy, and his eyes held a resigned look. He told no one of his problems, but went about his work as usual. That evening he opened the newspaper and read that "The Great White Fleet" of American Naval vessels had arrived in Virginia, having completed an around the world cruise begun in 1907. President Roosevelt had reviewed the fleet on its return. He leaned back in his chair and thought of his days on board the *Oregon* and the Battle for Santiago. He closed his eyes and slept, his newspaper spread across his chest.

He was suddenly awakened by pounding on his door. His housekeeper told him he was wanted at the hospital. He hadn't even heard the telephone ring. He went to the water closet and washed his face and hands, grabbed his medical bag and heavy winter coat and pulled his felt hat down hard on his ears against the cold. He took note of the ice in puddles on the street and walked carefully around them. He was grateful when he reached the safety of the warm building.

"Dr. Hadley, we're so grateful you could help out." Velma Willingham, a nurse who had started with Fuller on his day shift and recently taken over the night duties, held out a lined pad with a list of men's names. "You'll want to look over this before you head up to the surgery."

"Ah, thank you, Velma." Fuller shrugged off his coat, and she took the garment from him in a practiced manner. He accepted the list gratefully. "I see you've managed to get the people sorted out."

"You're welcome, Doctor. Now, this one." She pointed to one of the names on the list. "His name is Jarrod Pulaski. He was working on the railroads near Telluride. Apparently a buggy turned over . . . and well, it's rather bad."

"From a buggy accident?" Fuller frowned and looked at her. They were in the corridor by then, and he heard noise coming from around the corner. When they reached the junction, there were several men and two women wrapped in blankets, shivering, with several nurses comforting them. "What's this?"

"The other people on the list. We're sorting out their injuries now, but we think most of them are overly chilled or in emotional shock. We won't know about frostbite until we can get them sorted and examined more closely."

"Pulaski? Where is he?"

"Room 106. We had to get him in as quickly as possible. He was bleeding profusely. I said a buggy turned over. What I didn't get to was that he was racing the train. The train won, and he was dragged some fifty yards, witnesses said." She grimaced.

"Ah." Fuller took a deep breath. Probably a celebration that got out of hand, and this was the result. "Alright, let me get washed up." He made his way into the washroom and prepared for what he knew he was likely to find, expecting a very long night.

Fuller hoped he could save the man, but even amputation wasn't a life-saving option. The incident that had nearly removed his lower limb had done severe damage to his face, also, so his passing was probably a mercy. He would have been disfigured had he survived the operation. The man's companions wailed with grief, but there was nothing Fuller could have done, even if he'd gotten to him earlier.

Later that day, while a bleary-eyed and drained Fuller was eating a long-overdue lunch, William Howard Taft was sworn in as 27th President of the United States. There was a celebration in the doctor's lounge, but Fuller was too exhausted to care.

Twenty

Four years passed, the seasons slipping by faster and faster, with Fuller dividing his time between Denver and Sweetwater Station. He awoke one Saturday morning to the sound of a sledge hammer pounding wood.

"Damn hired hand," he muttered. "Why does he have to disturb the morning when people need to sleep?"

He rolled over and forced a pillow over his head, trying to fall back to sleep. The building aroma of coffee drifted into the room. After a few moments he sat up.

"Damn, coffee. How can I sleep with coffee tempting me out of bed?" He tossed the bedding aside, slipped into his house shoes and made his way to the bathroom. Unrolling his shaving kit, he caressed the gleaming straight razor, a recent purchase from a shop near his practice in Denver, and removed a bar of shaving soap to lather up his jaw. Placing it in a cup, he added a small amount of water and dropped in his shaving brush, letting it set for a moment, before swirling it around to work up a lather. Lifting it, he dabbed it on his face and grimaced at the pain in his hand. Raising his chin, he scraped the blade across his neck, continuing repeatedly until his face was smooth. He paused a moment and exercised his fingers until the cramp subsided enough to return his shaving paraphernalia to his kit. He dressed and went downstairs to the kitchen to find the housekeeper standing in front of a window shaking her head.

"Good morning, Corey. What going on?" Fuller peered out the glass to see if he could find what had her attention. The sharp report of a large hammer pounding against wood reverberated repeatedly.

She turned at the sound of his voice. "That fool. Doesn't he have sense enough to know that's what Rufus was hired for? Sit down, sir. Breakfast is almost ready." She turned from the window and poured him a cup of coffee, setting it on the table.

"Thanks, Corey." Fuller left the coffee and moved closer to the window to see what she was grumbling about. There was his father in his shirtsleeves swinging the hammer, one swift blow at a time. His shirt was already darkened with moisture. The large head was biting into wooden planks, not logs, as Fuller had suspected.

"Corey," Fuller called, glancing to see her at the stove. "What's my father doing?"

"Ask him. He never tells me anything." She didn't turn, but kept stirring a steaming pot.

Fuller opened the door and went outside. "Papa, what are you doing?" Joe didn't answer, so Fuller waited until his father finished knocking loose a square piece of board and spoke louder. "Papa. Stop for a while and rest."

"Good morning, son." Joe paused and laid the bulky hammer on a stack of lumber. He was breathing hard, and he pulled a white cloth from a pocket and wiped his forehead.

"What are you doing, Papa? What are these things?"

Joe picked one up and ran his hand over it, shaking his head. "You don't remember, do you? These are the molds with which Jeremiah Fuller and I made the brick barn. An Indian woman was here then, and she'd fill them with mud to dry in the sun."

"Rosie. I've heard the stories about that."

"Well, son. I looked around last night when everything was quiet and everybody was gone to bed and said to myself, what are we saving these molds for? We don't need them anymore; they're just stacked in the shed rotting away. Time to get some use out of them again." He pulled the handkerchief from his pocket and wiped his brow again. "Best thing to do is break them up for firewood, don't you think?"

Fuller burst out laughing. "Papa, you're incorrigible. Here, put that hammer back in the barn and come eat your breakfast. Corey's got hot coffee in the kitchen."

Joe looked at his son with a twinkle in his eyes. "Don't rightly know what that big word means, but I never turn down a cup of coffee when it's offered." He put his handkerchief in his pocket and strode to the back door of the house.

"If you really want those molds broken apart into firewood, why didn't you tell Rufus to do it?' Fuller held the door open so his father could go in ahead of him. "That's what you hired him for."

"Maybe. Maybe. But, sometimes a fellow just needs to do things for himself." He crossed to the sink, ignoring the presence of Corey and Fuller, and he washed his hands. He dried them on a dish cloth and sat down.

Corey emptied Fuller's cup and poured him another hot steaming cup of coffee, giving him a strange look, and set a cup down for Joe. The coffee smelled delicious, and Fuller took a sip. He looked up at Corey.

"He was breaking up the old brick molds." He watched as Joe leaned back in his chair, his cup in his hands.

"Brick molds?" She turned to bring the platter of bacon to the table. "Don't know nothing about brick molds, but how do you want your eggs, Fuller? Same as before?"

"Yes, bright yellow and hot."

"That's about what I thought." She laughed, went to the skillet and put it on the burner. Opening the ice box, she pulled out six eggs and closed the door.

"So, Papa, let's talk about what you were doing out there. Where's Rufus this morning? Milking the nannies? Is that why you didn't get him to break up the molds?" Fuller watched as Corey worked around the kitchen. She was quiet and efficient, but not as jolly as his Girtie, who did the cooking for him when he was in town. He took a piece of bacon and chewed it. It had gotten cold while he'd been outside. He reached for a biscuit; it also felt cold. He supposed it wasn't her fault; with Joe outside and him getting up later than usual, how was she expected to keep everything warm? He sighed.

"I haven't seen him this morning. He must be in the barn; the mule Hugo tried to break down the fence again. I'd get rid of that old stubborn soul if he wasn't such a good worker. It's always been that way; the mules and the goats want to wander into the forest or the desert. Looking for something they won't find, but too ignorant to know it." Joe picked up his fork and started to eat his eggs as soon as Corey put them on his plate. "Mmm, I'm hungry this morning."

"I wish someone would explain to me why you were out banging on wood so early in the morning; why, the sun ain't hardly over the treetops yet. And, what is this about brick molds? You never said." She slid his eggs onto Fuller's plate and stood there, giving him a glare that might have intimidated him if he were younger.

He heard the door slam and turned to see Franklin, dressed in overalls and a green-striped shirt. He looked like he'd been running, his face red and damp.

"Grandpa, Mama says what do you mean? Out there in the cold and dark, working before breakfast." He glanced at the bacon and sat down, taking a piece into his mouth. He looked up at Corey. "That's cold."

"Well, of course it's cold. How's a body to keep the food warm when everyone traipses in one at a time of a morning?" She set a cup on the table and poured it full of coffee. "Do you want eggs, or will you eat at your own place? Don't never know how many to cook for; people in and out like this was a fancy restaurant." She muttered to herself and picked up the platter of bacon and scraped them into the skillet to warm. She took a large cloth and pulled the pot of porridge off the burner and set it on the metal plate on the table. A stack of bowls and spoons were to the side. "There," she said. "That's hot. Help yourself, if you've a mind."

The door slammed again, and Corey groaned. This time it

was Rufus Blackburn, the hired man with a bucket of warm milk, straight from the nannies in the goat shed.

"Damn goat! Tried to knock over the bucket. If'n I hadn't caught it in time, wouldn't be no milk this mornin'. Beggin' your pardon, ma'am. Dr. Hadley, what you doing out beating on wood? Thought you was supposed to save your hands for the surgery. I'd get to making some firewood soon as I could, yes, I would. No need for you to work while you're here." He huffed and started to strain the milk of insects or dirt, mumbling to himself.

"It wasn't me this morning, Rufus. It was Papa."

The man turned so quickly he almost tipped over the bucket again. "Mr. Joe, now what you mean, working out in the yard? I ain't never seen a man so bent on killing hisself with work. You ain't got no call to be doing nothing so hard so early. I done said I'll get to it when I can."

"I know, Rufus. I'm sorry. I just got to thinking about those wooden molds and decided that now was the time to get rid of them." Joe sighed and finished his coffee. He spooned porridge into a bowl as he asked, "Corey, can you do me again? That coffee sure tastes good this morning." He took a spoonful of porridge into his mouth. "Is that bacon still fit to eat? I could use a couple of pieces."

With a moan, Corey dumped the warm bacon back onto the platter and slammed it on the table. She gave everyone a frustrated look and asked, "Franklin, do you want eggs or not? Gracious, with me with a ton of clothes washing to be done, and breakfast not even half started; and Rufus, you want eggs, too? If you do, you better collect some more."

"No, Corey, I don't want eggs. Thanks. Grandpa, Mama says to tell her if you need help with the chores, and she'll send Papa up to help." Franklin rose to leave. "I'd do it myself, but Lizzie wants me to dig up the taters and turnips in the garden this morning."

"Tell your mama that Walter doesn't need to come up. Rufus will get the work done when he can. Lordy, I didn't realize I was disturbing a hornet's nest when I dug out those rotten brick molds."

"There you are again. What brick molds you talking about?" Having strained the milk and poured it into a glass jug, and set it in the ice box, Rufus turned to Joe.

"Those old brick molds that Jeremiah Fuller and me used to build the barn. They've been sitting there in the supply shed taking up space all these many years, and I decided they'd make good firewood for this winter." Now everyone was staring at Joe with various expressions on their faces.

"Well, I never." Corey placed two eggs on a plate for Rufus. "That old barn? You made that yourself? When did you do that?" She sat down in one of the chairs, as though she couldn't handle any more surprises that morning. Franklin sat back down beside her.

Fuller laughed. "Papa, time to 'fess up. Tell us again how you and Buck Jones and Rosie and Jeremiah made the barn." He watched as Rufus ate his eggs, some bacon and a biscuit piled high with melted butter and honey. Franklin took a piece of bacon, and he reached for a biscuit for himself. He smeared it with honey, and a drop fell on the table. He took his finger and brought it to his mouth.

"It was in the first year that Hannah and I were here." Joe's eyes closed for a minute. He opened them and looked around. "It was so long ago; the year was 1866; the house was here and a few of the corrals, but we needed a barn. Buck Jones was the animal handler, and he had an Apache wife named Rosie. She made the bricks out of the clay and grass near the creek; hundreds of them." He turned and pointed, and although no one inside could see the creek, they knew where it was. "I made the molds, and she filled them. At first it was just me and Buck, then Jeremiah came to work as the hired hand." He stopped and coughed, and Fuller could see how even the memory of the man for whom he was named lingered in his father's mind.

"Go on, Papa. Tell us about the storm." Fuller watched the people at the table. The men had stopped eating and were gazing at Joe with awe.

"It was a terrible storm, the worst I've ever seen. The first wall was only half finished. Buck and I and Jeremiah took Buck's Conestoga and brought the logs from above the springs to make a shelter for the animals. We hammered and nailed, and barely had a roof on when the hail started. Large hail; the wind blew something fierce; two or three of those big trees fell down. But, the walls and the roof held it off." He laughed.

"The funniest thing was the chickens; Hannah and Rosie took them into one of the bedrooms, and they flew all over the room." He scratched his head in the gesture that was familiar to Fuller. "If I'd had my senses about me, we'd have put those chickens in the passageway, then Hannah wouldn't have had to clean the bedroom; but I was young and foolish then. Well, the hail and rain stopped, and we hauled those logs back to the place where the workers had left them. Was a ridiculous thing to do, for what did they become? The bunkhouse, that's what." He looked around him. "Everything on this place was made by hand, one building and corral at a time. And, now it's time for those brick molds to be useful again. May as well use them for firewood; they're just rotting away."

There was a moment of silence. The plates were still, no forks tinkled against knives and not even the sound of eating broke the pensive mood. Then, like a sudden breeze before a change in weather, arms and voices shifted into motion, and the room was filled with chatter and laughter.

"I gotta go; Mama will wonder what's keeping me. Thank you, Grandpa, for the story." And, Franklin ran out the door. Fuller rose and patted Joe on the shoulder.

"Papa, we'll see that the molds are chopped and stacked; come and help us. You can fetch and carry for us. Rufus?" With one more sigh of exasperation, Corey rose and began to clear the table. Rufus left without a word, and Fuller and Joe followed him to the shed where they brought out all the brick molds and lined them in a row near the woodpile.

With Joe taking a claw hammer to remove the nails in the molds, and Fuller, his hands enclosed in heavy leather gloves, working the sharpening stone when it was needed and carrying the wood to the pile near the back door, Rufus cut up molds until it was time to collect the eggs and go for the mail. It took them two days, but at last the pile of weathered, wooden molds were ready for the fireplace, and Joe Hadley was at peace.

Epilogue

Janey and Walter Abernathy moved into the larger house to accommodate their family group. Surprisingly, two of their boys, Franklin and Mark, remained on the farm, Franklin and his wife, Lizzie, living with his parents, while Mark and his family moved into the clapboard house near the river. The bunkhouse often rang with the laughter and antics of visitors from afar. The ice melted from around the edges of the spring, and the roses in Vanessa's garden bloomed in vibrant color.

Fuller hired a man named Curt Berry to help Rufus with the farm work. He and his wife, Sharlene, lived in the cabin Joe had built for his parents in 1869 after the wreck of the coach from Pueblo. It was modernized, and two rooms were added. The yard shrank with each addition, and a person would be hard pressed to imagine the way it was as Joe stepped out on a cool, spring morning and roused his coachmen with the pronouncement, "Coffee's hot."

Joe Hadley lived another thirteen years and was buried

beside Hannah, his boyhood friend, his wife and the mother of his children. The whole family but one came for the memorial service. They all looked to Fuller for guidance and comfort, and he didn't fail them. The eulogy was short, for they all knew the story so well, of the young man and woman who left Indiana shortly after the war and rode the steamboats and stage to the home in the forest that Joe Hadley carved out of the wilderness with his own hands.

Fuller moved into the station house and slept in the first bedroom behind the fireplace where he was born. He made a few changes: shelves for his books, and a polished wood bar for his whiskeys and malts; but basically the house remained as it was built by Clifton Taylor and Odell Graham of the Overland Stage Line. He didn't marry again but spent his life as he had always lived, gambling, womanizing, drinking and in service to others as his father and mother had before him. When he was in his fifties he was forced to retire from his profession and sat for hours with Janey or Gloria, pen in hand, and started a long, rambling tome about the history of the medical profession. When his hands began to twist up, and he could no longer put his words on paper, he gave up on his writing.

"It's over," Fuller cursed on the day he could no longer hold his pen. He threw the instrument across the room, disgusted at the barely legible scribble that covered his tablet.

Gloria set the lunch tray on a side table, and she picked up the pen, handing it back to him. "Uncle, you've got so much to tell. Why don't you take a break and have some of Mama's lamb chops? Then perhaps you'll feel like writing just a little more."

"With these hands?" He held them up to expose the gnarled digits attached to each one.

"Perhaps I could take notes for you?" She smiled encouragingly.

"I appreciate your offer, but you and I both know I need someone who can write as fast as I can talk." Fuller pushed the pen away. "I'd become a burden to you, and you'd come to hate it. You need to be outside on your horse, not in here with an old man."

"No, Uncle!" Gloria put her hand on his arm. "I'd never hate the time I spent with you."

"I love you, but no, it's best I put the writing aside." Fuller stood and shuffled to the window, looking at the mountains rising above the tree tops. He worked the joints on his right hand between the fingers of his left to ease the pain.

Janey was the one who put together a solution, turning up several days later with Philly, the clinic nurse, and a brown case in hand.

"Brother, I have an answer to our problem." She was bright and cheerful. Although in her early fifties, she'd retained her smooth skin and youthful figure, belying a woman old enough to be a grandmother. She laughed and pulled Philly to stand before her.

"Our problem?" Fuller closed his old journal from his war years aboard the *Oregon* and placed one gnarled hand on the cover. Her words irritated him. "Mine, you mean."

"Our problem." She drew close and put her hands on either side of his face. "We're family, and we work out our solutions together. You've a story to tell, and I want you to tell it. Philly

237

is going to help you."

"She is, is she?" He looked at her critically. "She's a nurse. Don't need no damned nurse, not till I'm ready to die. Not dying yet, Sister." He held the sheaf of journaled and bound papers clutched in one twisted hand, and he shook it at her. His fingers lost their grip, and he dropped it loudly to the floor.

"Of course not." She patted his cheek and kissed him on the forehead. "You're not finished writing, either. Philly?"

"Here, Dr. Hadley. Septimus gave me two days and the weekend. He told me he can get along just fine in the clinic for that long, and I can do what I originally trained to do." She had the case on a table, and she unsnapped the latches. She lifted the lid to expose a black, Underwood typewriter with three rows of white keys. She lifted it from the lower half of the case and set it to the side, closing the case and settling it onto a sideboard out of the way.

"You expect me to use that?" Fuller looked at Janey and winked. He was beginning to understand.

"Come, now, Dr. Hadley." Philly made a tutting sound, but she smiled. "I will have you know, I was quite a receptionist in my younger days. My fingers still work very well, and I'm pretty certain I can keep up with you, no matter how fast you want to ramble on about nothing."

"You think she can, Janey?" He said it with a twinkle in his eyes.

Janey's answer was to pull out several reams of paper and set them on the table beside the typewriter. She picked up the journal of his war years on the ship *Oregon*, and with a solemn glare, she placed it close at hand. Philly ripped the end of a package of paper and pulled out two sheets, placed a sheet of carbon between them, and slipped them into the typewriter. She twisted the carriage until it was aligned. She pulled up a chair, poised her hands over the keys, and she intoned with mock drama, "Ready when you are, Doctor."

Fuller began to talk, and Philly's fingers flew across the keys. The wind blew through the windows, rustling the curtains, and as the papers beside the typewriter began to fill with the words of a lifetime, the sun sank behind the horizon, and the glow of electric lights brushed the lawn beyond the sturdy walls of the station house. It was well after midnight when they shut it down that first night, but Fuller was satisfied with their progress. His tale was on its way to being told. He might not have children of his own, but his sister's children and his brother's children would know the events of his life. He'd tell it all, and the parts that weren't as exciting as he liked, well, he was telling the story, and it would say exactly what he wanted it to say.

Fuller Hadley did finish his story, with the support of the women who helped him make the most of his final days. He died at the age of fifty-eight and was buried among the pine trees and spruce of his home.

And, still the mountains can be seen in the late evening shadows, eagles fly high over the meadows and the coyotes wail at the full moon. The night winds whistle through the eaves and shuttered windows of the old station house, and the cool, clear waters of the spring flow gently into the creek as it makes it way down to the river and eventually to the sea.